LUC & FRANÇOIS

THE HOLLOW GROUNDS

LUC SCHUITEN, Writer
FRANÇOIS SCHUITEN, Artist
JULIA SOLIS, Translation

THIERRY FRISSEN,
Book Design

PATRICK LEHANCE,
Letterer

PAUL BENJAMIN,
Editor, Collected Edition

SUSAN M. GARRETT,
Assistant Editor, Collected Edition

BRUNO LECIGNE & FABRICE GIGER,
Editors, Original Edition

DC COMICS:
PAUL LEVITZ, President & Publisher
GEORG BREWER, VP-Design & Retail Product Development
RICHARD BRUNING, Senior VP-Creative Director
PATRICK CALDON, Senior VP-Finance & Operations
CHRIS CARAMALIS, VP-Finance
TERRI CUNNINGHAM, VP-Managing Editor
ALISON GILL, VP-Manufacturing
RICH JOHNSON, VP-Book Trade Sales
HANK KANALZ, VP-General Manager, WildStorm
LILLIAN LASERSON, Senior VP & General Counsel
JIM LEE, Editorial Director-WildStorm
DAVID MCKILLIPS, VP-Advertising & Custom Publishing
JOHN NEE, VP-Business Development
GREGORY NOVECK, Senior VP-Creative Affairs
CHERYL RUBIN, Senior VP-Brand Management
BOB WAYNE, VP-Sales & Marketing

THE HOLLOW GROUNDS
Humanoids Publishing. PO Box 931658, Hollywood. CA 90094.
This is a publication of DC Comics, 1700 Broadway. New York. NY 10019.

THE FLITTERS TAKE OFF FROM THE GREAT WALL. 36° LATITUDE, 3° LONGITUDE, 979 PERIODS, 76 LUMBARS/FREQUENCY 179

MATERIALIZING FREQUENCY 207 TO 210 Ω	POSITION 53° LATITUDE 4° LONGITUDE	UNIVERSAL TIME 979 PERIODS 787 LUMBARS

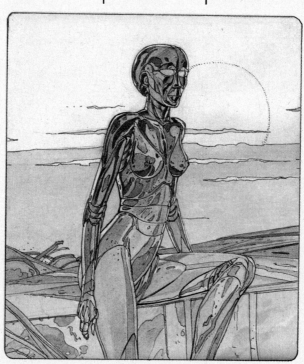

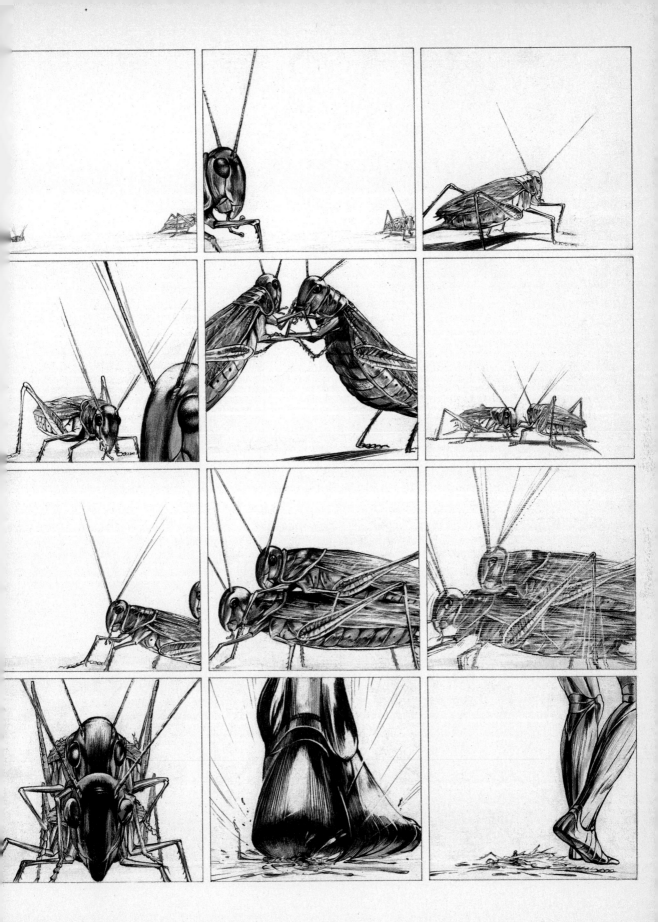

AAHH...
THIS *DAMN* MACHINE
NEVER WORKS!

WE *CAN'T* GO ON LIKE THIS!
IT MUST STILL BE POSSIBLE TO
CONNECT THE WAY PEOPLE *USED* TO...

NO WAY! YOU KNOW THAT'S IMPOSSIBLE!
IT'S MUCH TOO DANGEROUS...

LOOK AT THE TILOMETER. IT'S 25
ARTOSE DEGREES BELOW ZERO... THAT HASN'T
HAPPENED FOR AT LEAST 25 LUMBARS!

YES, BUT THAT COULD CHANGE AT ANY MOMENT.
AND WHAT ABOUT THE *INSECTS?*

THEY'RE ASLEEP AT THIS HOUR... WE CAN RISK IT.

MAYBE. BUT IT'S VERY DANGEROUS.
REMEMBER WHAT HAPPENED THAT OTHER TIME?

WHAT ARE
YOU DOING?
YOU'RE
INSANE!

YOUR REAL EYES... YOUR MOUTH! IT'S DISGUSTING... AND YET FASCINATING!

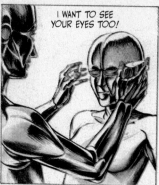

I WANT TO SEE YOUR EYES TOO!

YOUR LIPS!

I CAN'T BELIEVE IT! SUCH SOFT SKIN, ALWAYS *HIDDEN*... AND I'M TOUCHING IT FOR THE FIRST TIME!

I'M SO EXCITED IT'S ALMOST SICKENING!

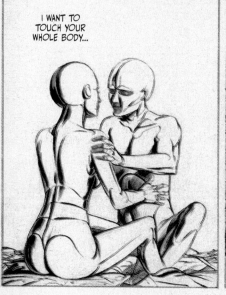

I WANT TO TOUCH YOUR WHOLE BODY...

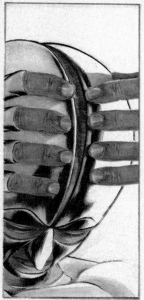

NO!

THE GREAT MIGRATION OF FLITTERS ON A SOUTHBOUND EXODUS. HERE THEY ARE CROSSING THE ENDLESS
DESERT EXPANSE. 51.2° LATITUDE 4.4° LONGITUDE / UNIVERSAL TIME 979 PERIODS - 787 LUMBARS

STAMPEDE

MATERIALIZING FREQUENCY 301 TO 320 Ω	POSITION 49° LATITUDE 5° LONGITUDE	UNIVERSAL TIME 979 PERIODS 789 LUMBARS

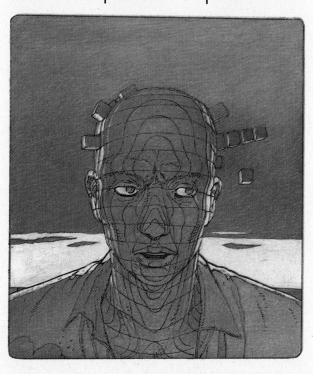

STAMPEDE

WAIT, I'M COMING
DOWN...

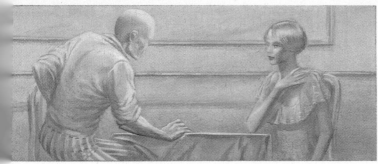

YOUR HAIR KNOT... WHAT A *TEMPTATION*...

...ES, BUT IF YOU TOUCH IT...

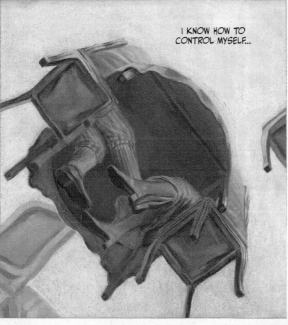

I KNOW HOW TO CONTROL MYSELF...

REALLY? YOU ALWAYS SEEM TO WORK YOURSELF INTO A STATE...

YOU SEE...? YOU'RE DOING IT AGAIN...

THAT'S HARSH! YOU'RE THE ONE WHO DOES THIS TO ME EVERY TIME...

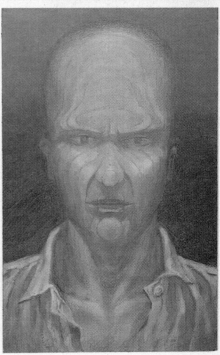

DON'T EXPECT ME TO WATCH *THIS...*

WAIT! DON'T JUST LEAVE ME LIKE THIS...

SIR, SOME OF OUR PATRONS ARE DISTURBED BY YOUR BEHAVIOR... THERE ARE ESTABLISHMENTS WHO CATER TO THAT SORT OF THING...

ALL RIGHT, I GET THE MESSAGE.

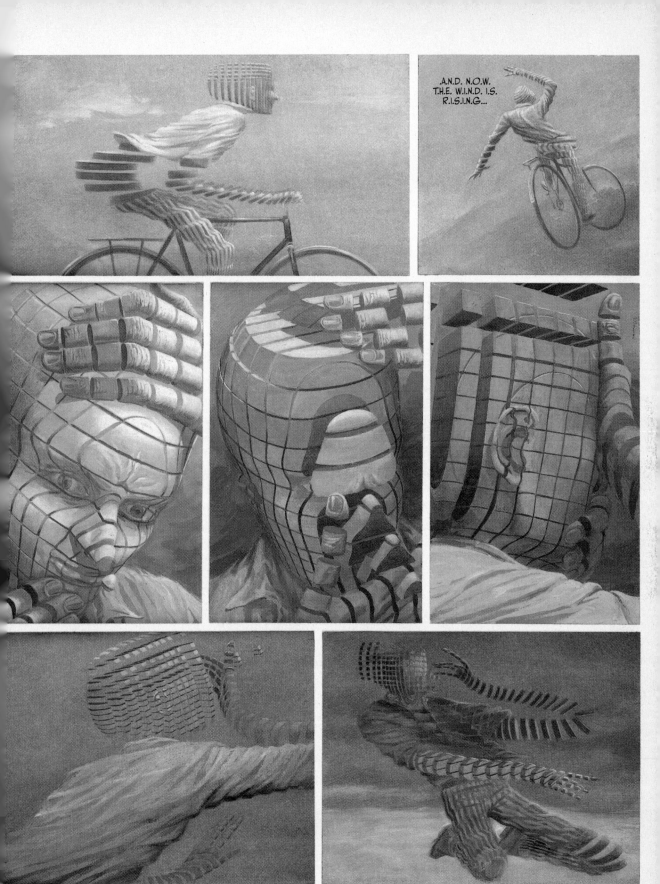

THE FLITTERS ARE MOVING FROM A 301/320 _ FREQUENCY TO ONE OF 679/683 _ THESE QUASI-MYTHIC CREATURES ARE THE ONLY BEINGS IN THE UNIVERSE KNOWN TO BE ABLE TO MOVE FROM ONE MATERIALIZING FREQUENCY TO ANOTHER.

CREVICE

MATERIALIZING FREQUENCY 679 TO 683 Ω	POSITION 45° LATITUDE 3° LONGITUDE	UNIVERSAL TIME 979 PERIODS 810 LUMBARS

SEE THAT? OUR NEWLYWEDS STILL DON'T HAVE A NUPTUAL BED.

WE DON'T NEED ONE. NATURE WILL BE OUR BED.

HA-HA!

HA-HA!

JEANNETTE?!

DON'T JUST STAND THERE... STOP THE RAVINE FROM CLOSING UP AGAIN!

THERE'S *NOTHING* WE CAN DO.

HURRY! HURRY!

I'M GOING DOWN.

SOMEONE HOLD ON TO THE HANDLE!

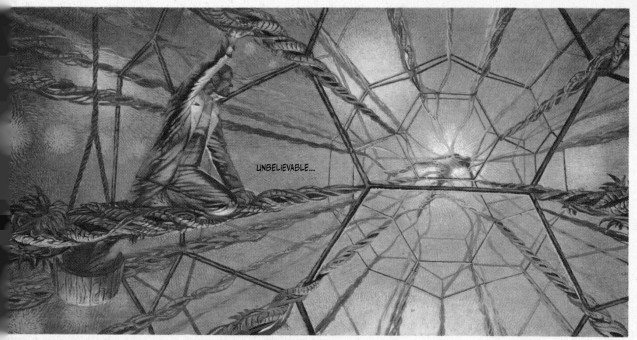

UNBELIEVABLE...

LET HER GO!

DAMNED BIO-ROBOT! HE'S GONE COMPLETELY MAD!!

HE'LL LEARN TO DO WHAT HE'S TOLD... OR ELSE!

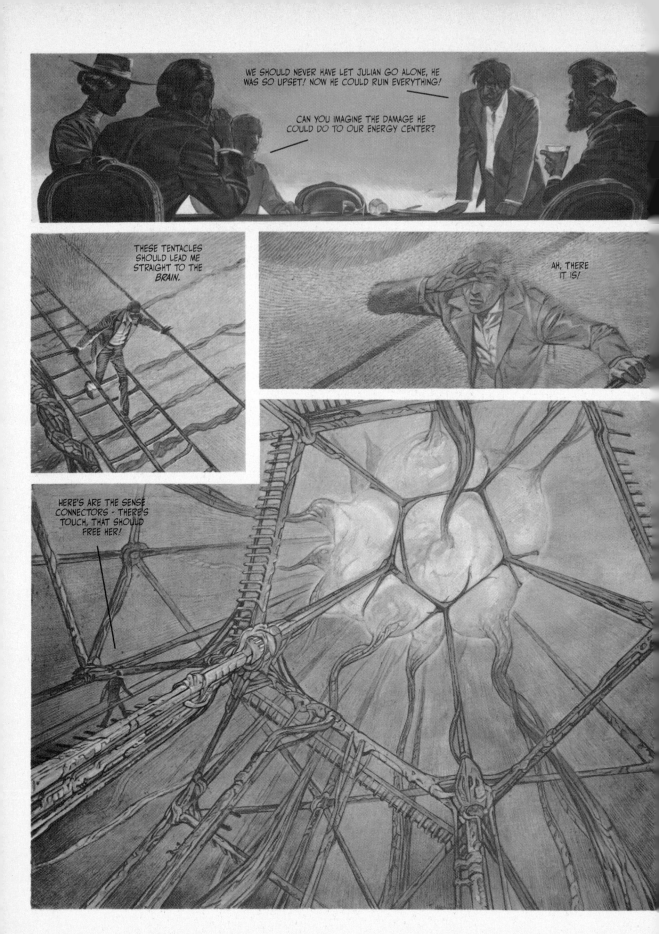

I'LL DISCONNECT ALL OF THEM...

BZZZZZZZZ...

GLIP

STOP! IF YOU DISCONNECT MY TENTACLES, JEANNETTE WILL PLUMMET TO THE BOTTOM!

OH *NO!* HE'S RIGHT!

CALM DOWN! I'M GOING TO SET YOUR WIFE DOWN ON THE CATWALK. SHE HASN'T BEEN HARMED - I ONLY CARESSED HER.

ONLY?!

FORGIVE ME, I COULDN'T HELP MYSELF. I'VE CREATED A GIFT FOR YOU BOTH, TO MAKE UP FOR WHAT I DID...

I DON'T WANT YOUR GIFT, YOU *SEX-CRAZED* ROBOT!

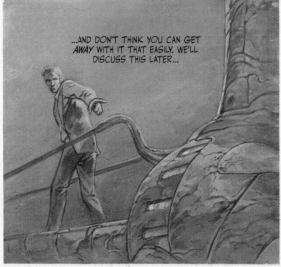

...AND DON'T THINK YOU CAN GET *AWAY* WITH IT THAT EASILY. WE'LL DISCUSS THIS LATER...

OOOOH...

DOING THIS TO US ON OUR WEDDING DAY... WHAT'S GOTTEN INTO HIM?

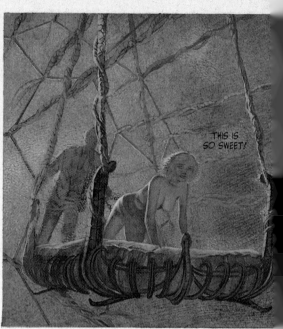

THE CONTROL CENTER'S REACTION MAKES SENSE. ITS BRAIN HASN'T BEEN ABLE TO ADJUST TO THE LACK OF CONTACT WITH HUMAN FLESH.

WE HAVE TO HELP HIM. AFTER ALL, WE OWE HIM OUR LIVES. HE PROVIDES US WITH OUR ENERGY. WE MUST FIND A SOLUTION.

HA HA! DON'T YOU GET IT - HE'S ALREADY FOUND THE SOLUTION! DIDN'T YOU *NOTICE* THE BED?

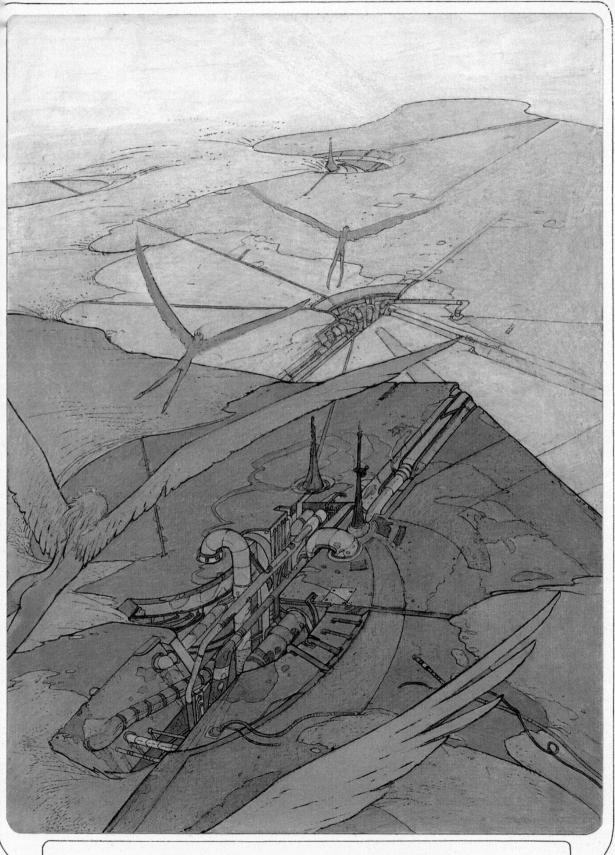

A GROUP OF FLITTERS FLIES OVER AN ENERGY CENTER. 59° LATITUDE -
3° LONGITUDE/FREQUENCY 680... IT'S UNUSUAL TO SEE THEM WITH THE NAKED EYE: THEY ALMOST
NEVER CROSS OVER INTO THE FREQUENCIES AT WHICH OUR UNIVERSE MATERIALIZES.

SAMPLE

MATERIALIZING FREQUENCY 369 TO 372 Ω	POSITION 59° LATITUDE 3° LONGITUDE	UNIVERSAL TIME 980 PERIODS 02 LUMBARS

TARGET LOCATED...

...TRACTOR BEAM...SAMPLE...ANIMAL IDENTIFIED...

...RECOVERY COMPLETED...

A GROUP OF FLITTERS PREPARING TO TOUCH DOWN AT DUSK, BEYOND THE 46TH PARALLEL.
NOTICE THE DIFFICULTIES IN OBTAINING THIS TYPE OF PHOTO: THE FLITTERS DON'T APPEAR IN
THE PHOTOGRAPHER'S VISUAL RANGE, LIMITING HIM TO WORKING IN THE DARK. THEY WILL ONLY
BECOME VISIBLE AFTER THE PROOFS HAVE BEEN DEVELOPED.

EXPLANATORY NOTES ON THE
VILLAGE OF FOG.

CURRENT TECHNOLOGY ENABLES EVERY HOUSE TO BE HEATED BY SOLAR
ENERGY, EVEN DURING THE UNFAVORABLE CONDITIONS OF THE WINTER
SOLSTICE. DURING EXTENDED PERIODS OF SUNLESS DAYS, AN ENERGY
CENTER STOCKED WITH CALORIES IS PLACED BENEATH THE TOWN SQUARE.
AN EOLIAN, WHOSE MAST IS COVERED WITH SOLAR CAPACITORS, CONTAINS
THE BATTERIES FOR STORING SOLAR ELECTRICITY, BIO-MASS TREATMENT
INSTALLATIONS, AND THE GAZOGENE. IN THE CENTER OF THE TOWN
SQUARE, THREE MULTI-FACETED PRISMS TRAVEL THE LENGTH OF THE
GRADED MAST, THUS INFORMING THE TOWNSPEOPLE OF THEIR ENERGY
RESERVES. ONCE THE THREE PRISMS REACH THE TOP OF THE MAST, THE
SUN RAYS THAT SUCCESSIVELY PIERCE THEM WILL CREATE A SPHERICAL
RAINBOW, ENVELOPING THE ENTIRE TOWN INSIDE A DOME. THIS SIGNALS
THE BEGINNING OF THE FOLK FESTIVITIES, WHICH LAST SEVERAL CYCLES.

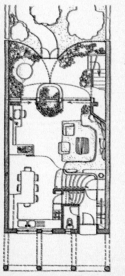

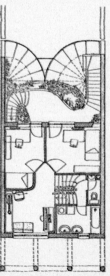

HOMES ARE SELF-
CONSTRUCTED UNDER
THE SUPERVISION OF
A MASTER MASON.
STABILIZED SOIL, THE
PRINCIPAL MATERIAL IN
THEIR CONSTRUCTION
IS SO EASY TO USE
THAT THE ENTIRE FAMILY
PARTICIPATES IN THE
CREATION AND
CONSTRUCTION OF
THEIR PERSONAL
HABITAT.

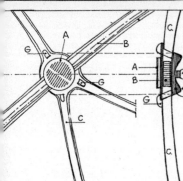

INCISION IN THE STRUCTURE'S CORE

IN SUMMER, THE DETACHABLE GREENHOUSES ACT AS NATURAL, SELF-REGULATING CLIMATE CONTROLS, ALSO ENABLING PLANTS TO GROW. THEY CAPTURE SOLAR ENERGY, STORING IT IN INERT THERMOSES OF STABILIZED EARTH. THE GREENHOUSES CONSIST OF A PLASTIC FILM THAT ISOLATES A HEAT MIRROR, SET INSIDE A PLIABLE FIBERGLASS STRUCTURE (B) AND KEPT OPEN BY MEDIANS (C) ATTACHED TO THE MAIN STRUCTURE (B) BY MEANS OF A CORE CONTAINING A SOLAR PHOTOCELL (A). THE LATTER CHARGES A BATTERY (F), WHICH LIGHTS A SMALL INNER LAMP (D) PLACED AT THE CENTER OF A PARABOLIC MIRROR (E). THESE LAMPS LIGHT UP ONLY AFTER DARK AND KEEP THE GREENHOUSES ILLUMINATED FOR SEVERAL HOURS.

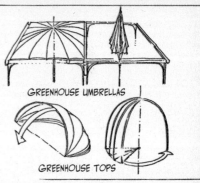

GREENHOUSE UMBRELLAS

GREENHOUSE TOPS

SOUTH FACADE OF THE GREENHOUSE

SOUTH FACADE WITH OPEN GREENHOUSE

NORTH FACADE

THE FOG CUTTER

MATERIALIZING FREQUENCY 1012 TO 1020 Ω	POSITION 44.5° LATITUDE 5.6° LONGITUDE	UNIVERSAL TIME 980 PERIODS 07 LUMBARS

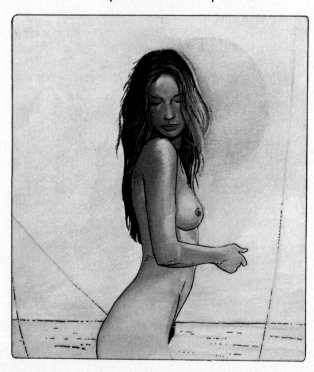

THE FOG CUTER

...HED FOR
...ODAY.

I HOPE SHE'S
NOT UP YET...

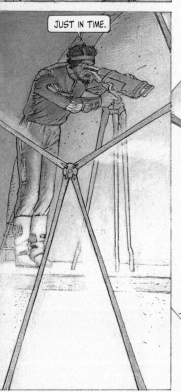

JUST IN TIME.

OH DEAR, IT'S ALREADY [FOG]GY! I SHOULD HAVE WORN [S]OMETHING WARMER...

HMM... HE'S ON TIME.

HELLO, RUDOLPH!

THERE THEY GO!

YOU'RE BAD, RUDOLPH!

...YOU DON'T FEEL LIKE TASTING MY FAMOUS ORBEDALD LIQUEUR?

THE FOLLOWING MORNING...

OH, RUDOLPH, LOOK... THE FOG! IT'S *SOLIDIFIED*.

WHAT? AT THIS TIME OF YEAR?

THAT'LL KEEP YOUR CUTTER BUSY. AT LEAST HE'LL LEAVE YOU ALONE FOR A WHILE.

ON THE SOLIDIFIED FOG...

INCREDIBLE! AND IN THE MIDDLE OF THE HARVEST. WHAT IS THE WORLD COMING TO?

THEY CAN'T CONVINCE ME THIS HAS NOTHING TO DO WITH THEIR ECOLOGICAL EXPERIMENTS.

LOOK, SHE WAS CAUGHT BY SUR-PRISE LAST NIGHT. SHE'S A PRISONER! POOR THING! AT HER AGE...

SHE'S LUCKY THE CUTTER CAN SET HER FREE IN NO TIME.

NOW, DON'T MOVE! I HAVE OTHER THINGS TO DO.

YOU'RE VERY SWEET, CUTTER...

A THOUSAND KALAKS! WHY DO YOU ALL INSIST ON SLEEPING WITH YOUR GREENHOUSE OPEN? COME ON! YOU CAN FREE YOUR ARM NOW...

HE HAS SUCH A TEMPER!

THERE WE ARE, MRS. TOUSSIN, IT'S ALL OVER.

NOW TO THE NEXT ONE.

OH, DEAR! WE HAVEN'T SEEN THIS SINCE THE FAMOUS SOLIDIFYING OF ZERO THIRTEEN.

CUTTER, PLEASE DON'T FORGET TO COME BACK AND FREE A FEW CHAIRS FOR ME. I HAVE NOTHING TO SIT ON...

YEAH, WE'LL SEE, WE'LL SEE...

LOOK WHO'S HERE.

HEY, CUTTER, NOW THAT YOU'RE THE MOST IMPORTANT MAN IN TOWN, YOU DON'T SAY HELLO. YOU'RE NOT INTERESTED IN ME ANYMORE?

BUT I... I...

DON'T MIND HER, SHE'S JUST A TEASE.

HURRY UP! PEOPLE ARE WAITING FOR YOU!

BY THE FOLLOWING DAY, ANOTHER LAYER OF FOG HAS BEEN DEPOSITED AND SOLIDIFIED ACROSS THE TOWN...

GOOD GOD!

49

NO, NO *AND NO!* GO AWAY! I'M ALMOST DONE!

BUT, CUTTER, EVERYONE IS WAITING FOR YOU.

WE CAN'T DO ANYTHING WITHOUT YOU!

I ONLY HAVE TO ASSEMBLE IT. I'LL HELP YOU TOMORROW, IF YOU LIKE...

...THEY JUST HAVE TO CLOSE THEIR WINDOWS AT NIGHT!

BUT THE LAST LAYER TRAPPED A LOT OF PEOPLE. WE WEREN'T EXPECTING IT.

YOU'RE THE ONLY ONE IN TOWN, CUTTER... IT'S YOUR DUTY...

HE HAD TO OPEN HIS DOME TO BUILD THAT THING. WHERE IS THIS OBSESSION GOING TO END?

HE'S GONE MAD!

I DON'T GIVE A DAMN ABOUT YOUR PROBLEMS!

YOU'LL SEE, THIS WON'T TAKE LONG.

PIERRETTE AND HER NEIGHBOR WERE TRAPPED IN HER BED BY THE SOLIDIFICATION... HER HUSBAND IS GOING CRAZY. WE WON'T BE ABLE TO CONTROL HIM MUCH LONGER. YOU HAVE TO FREE THEM IMMEDIATELY...

WHERE'S THE CUTTER?!

...AH, HERE HE IS. NOT A MOMENT TOO SOON! IS THERE ANYONE LEFT IN TOWN WHO HASN'T STOPPED BY?

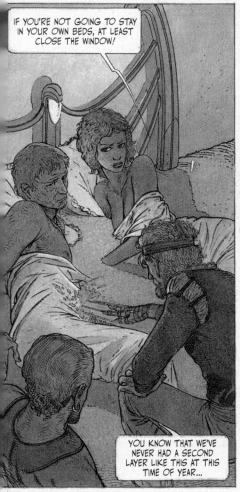

IF YOU'RE NOT GOING TO STAY IN YOUR OWN BEDS, AT LEAST CLOSE THE WINDOW!

YOU KNOW THAT WE'VE NEVER HAD A SECOND LAYER LIKE THIS AT THIS TIME OF YEAR...

LATER...

I'M DONE. EVERYONE IS RELEASED.

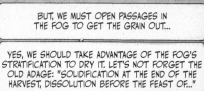

BUT, WE MUST OPEN PASSAGES IN THE FOG TO GET THE GRAIN OUT...

YES, WE SHOULD TAKE ADVANTAGE OF THE FOG'S STRATIFICATION TO DRY IT. LET'S NOT FORGET THE OLD ADAGE: "SOLIDIFICATION AT THE END OF THE HARVEST, DISSOLUTION BEFORE THE FEAST OF..."

AFTER ANOTHER DAY'S WORK OUTSIDE....
THE CUTTER HAS BEEN BUSY ALL NIGHT...

...I HAVE TO MAKE UP
FOR LOST TIME...

...EVERY YEAR IT'S
THE SAME THING!

...THEY ALWAYS COUNT ON ME
TO FIX THEIR MISTAKES...

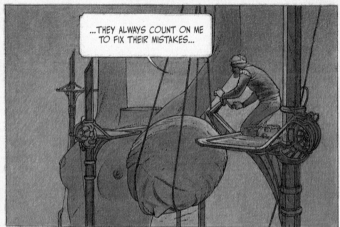

HUH?

OH NO!

THIS CAN'T BE HAPPENING... A NEW LAYER IS ABOUT TO SOLIDIFY. THE THIRD ONE...

THIS TIME I KNOW WHAT I'LL DO! THEY'RE NOT GOING TO FIND ME AGAIN...

FIRST, CLEAR THE AREA AROUND THE STATUE...

GOOD, THE FOG HASN'T QUITE THICKENED YET...

...THEN BLOCK THE ACCESS STAIRS.

NOW...URSULINE!!

FREE URSULINE!

?!

ONCE THE FOG HAS SOLIDIFIED...

MMM... BUT WHO IS...

WONDERFUL... WONDERFUL...

YOU'RE COMPLETELY INSANE! YOU BURY ME IN THE MIDDLE OF THE NIGHT IN SOLIDIFIED FOG AND YOU THINK THAT'S WONDERFUL?

ABSOLUTELY FANTASTIC. I'VE BEEN DREAMING OF THIS FOR YEARS... IT'S A HUNDRED TIMES BETTER THAN I COULD HAVE DONE IT MYSELF...

WHAT A PERFECT MOLD. THE SKIN IN ALL ITS FINEST DETAILS.

THAT'S *ENOUGH!* YOU'RE GOING TO FIX THIS MESS RIGHT NOW. LOOK AT MY BEDROOM. THERE'S FOG EVERYWHERE.

FIRST I WANT YOU TO CLEAR THAT CORNER.

WHAT LUCK, THE MOLD IS INTACT!

SOME OF THE FOG STILL HASN'T HARDENED. I HAVE EVERYTHING I NEED...

HEY, WHAT ARE YOU DOING? I WANT YOU TO CLEAR MY STAIRS RIGHT NOW!

YOU CAN'T JUST LEAVE! NOT AFTER YOU'VE BLOCKED EVERYTHING. I'M TRAPPED UP HERE!

THIS MATERIAL IS PERFECT FOR A QUICK-SET MOLD...

HE DOESN'T GIVE A DAMN ABOUT ME...

LISTEN, CUTTER, I GOT A LITTLE UPSET. YOU KNOW, IF YOU COME BACK AND SET ME FREE, I WON'T BE ANGRY WITH YOU ANYMORE.

AN HOUR LATER...

OKAY, I GOT CARRIED AWAY, I ADMIT IT. BUT YOU'RE ALSO TO BLAME... LET'S FORGET EVERYTHING AND YOU TAKE CARE OF MY STAIRS...

HEY, COME ON, DID YOU HEAR ME?

RECENT STUDIES OF THESE NEW DOCUMENTS HAVE LED TO A NUMBER OF DISCOVERIES...

ONE OF THE MOST IMPORTANT IS UNQUESTIONABLY THE MATERIALIZATION OF FLITTERS IN DOZENS, EVEN HUNDREDS OF UNIVERSES AS A CONSEQUENCE OF THEIR IN-FLIGHT COPULATION.

OLIVE

PERSONAL DIARY
EPOCH 139 27TH CYCLE 13TH PERIOD

I'M TIRED OF BEING TREATED LIKE A CHILD.
AFTER ALL, I'M NOW MORE THAN 65 CYCLES OLD.
MANY OTHERS HAVE BEEN INITIATED BEFORE MY AGE.
EVERY TIME I QUESTION THEM, THE ELDERS TELL
ME THAT WE HAVE TO BE WELL AHEAD OF OUR
SCHEDULE BEFORE WE CAN STOP FOR THREE ENTIRE
PERIODS FOR THE INITIATION FESTIVITIES...

IT'S DIFFICULT TO GET AHEAD OF OUR SCHEDULE, SINCE THAT WOULD MAKE OUR WALKING TOO STRENUOUS. THE CARRIAGES NO LONGER MOVE ON THEIR OWN. PUSHING THEM IS REALLY HARD AND THE WHOLE TRIBE HAS TO PARTICIPATE. WHEN WE STOP FOR THREE PERIODS, IT'S JUST THE OPPOSITE - THE CARRIAGES TAKE OFF BY THEMSELVES AND MUST BE HELD BACK. THAT'S EVEN HARDER, BECAUSE WE'RE SO TIRED AFTER THE FEAST.

21ST PERIOD

I WOULD LIKE TO KNOW WHY WE HAVE TO WALK ALL DAY LONG, ONLY TO RETURN TO OUR STARTING POINT AT THE END OF EACH CYCLE. WHY IS THERE ALWAYS THIS FEAR THAT WE HAVEN'T COVERED ENOUGH GROUND?

MY FRIENDS ASK THEMSELVES THE SAME QUESTIONS: WHY MUST WE ALWAYS ADVANCE AT THE SAME SPEED AS THE WATER IN THE LAKE? WHY DOES OUR PATRIARCH ALWAYS FOLLOW THE LITTLE RAFT AND NEVER TAKE HIS EYES OFF IT? WHAT IS SO TERRIBLE THAT MAKES US THIS AFRAID?

24TH PERIOD

THE INITIATED KNOW, BUT THEY WON'T TELL US ANYTHING. ARE WE BEING STALKED BY A MORTAL ENEMY? A MONSTER WHO DEVOURS THOSE WHO LAG BEHIND?

26TH PERIOD

MAYBE THEY DON'T KNOW...
THEY'VE NEVER DONE ANYTHING BUT RUN AWAY.
NOBODY HAS EVER HAD THE COURAGE TO STAY IN
ONE PLACE. AND YET THE TREES AND FLOWERS
DON'T CHANGE LOCATIONS AND NOTHING BAD HAPPENS
TO THEM. ON THE CONTRARY, WHEN WE FIND THEM
ON THE FOLLOWING CYCLE, THE SEEDS HAVE BECOME
LARGE PLANTS READY FOR HARVESTING.

27TH PERIOD

NOW I JUST
HAVE TO KNOW! I'LL BE THE ONE
WHO FINDS OUT THE TRUTH. I'LL
MAKE NOTES IN MY JOURNAL OF
EVERYTHING THAT HAPPENS TO ME,
AND I'LL HIDE IT AT THE FOOT
OF THE GREAT BAHOO TREE.

THAT WAY, IF SOMETHING BAD HAPPENS
TO ME, EVERYONE WILL FINALLY KNOW
WHAT REALLY GOES ON BEHIND US.

28TH PERIOD

THEY'VE LEFT...
THEY STILL DON'T KNOW THAT I STAYED
HERE. I KNOW THEY'LL NEVER COME BACK
FOR ME. THEY CAN'T RETRACE THEIR STEPS.
FREEDOM! FOR THE FIRST TIME IN MY LIFE
I AM TRULY FREE! I'M NO LONGER
FORCED TO WALK.

BEFORE THEY LEFT, I TOOK A LARGE BAG OF
BALIK GRAIN, SOME BISCUITS AND DRIED FRUIT.
I ALSO HAVE TWO FULL SKINS OF DRINKING WATER.
I CAN SURVIVE AT LEAST A WHOLE CYCLE. FROM THE
TOP OF MY TREE I'LL SEE THEM COMING. THEY WON'T
BELIEVE THEIR EYES... NOW I CAN WATCH THE SCENERY
FOR AS LONG AS I LIKE. I'M GOING TO TAKE
ALL THE TIME I WANT.

I AM THE FIRST
TO DISCOVER THE WORLD
FROM A FIXED POINT.

29TH PERIOD

MY FIRST NIGHT ALONE. SLEEPING ON THE GROUND IS UNCOMFORTABLE. I HAD BECOME ACCUSTOMED TO THE CARRIAGE'S ROCKING. HERE EVERYTHING IS QUIET. I CAN EVEN HEAR MY HEART BEATING.

SOMETHING HAS CHANGED.

NO DOUBT ABOUT IT, THE GROUND IS SLANTING MORE AND
MORE. IS THAT THE REASON FOR OUR FORCED MARCH?

30TH PERIOD

I'M VERY AFRAID.
THE SILENCE IS
DEAFENING. IT'S TOO LATE
TO JOIN THE OTHERS.

34TH PERIOD

SINCE THIS MORNING
THERE HAS BEEN NO WATER IN THE LAKE.
THE LANDSCAPE HAS BECOME TERRIFYING.
I'M AFRAID MORE AND MORE ALL THE TIME.

42ND PERIOD

THE GROUND'S INCLINATION IS INCREASING STEADILY. TODAY I ALMOST FELL DOWN THE ENTIRE SLOPE; I WOULD'VE REACHED THE BOTTOM IN LITTLE PIECES. STONES CONTINUALLY COME LOOSE AND ROLL DOWN, MAKING QUITE A RACKET. THAT KEEPS ME FROM SLEEPING.

I'M SO AFRAID. I'LL NEVER MAKE IT TO THE END OF THE CYCLE.

78TH PERIOD

TODAY I'M HALFWAY
THROUGH THE CYCLE. NOW I WILL
START MOVING DOWNWARD AGAIN.
THE WORST IS OVER. I'M NOT AS
SCARED AS I WAS SINCE I MADE A
FRIEND. HE LOVES MY BALIK SEEDS...

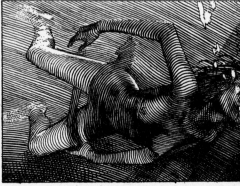

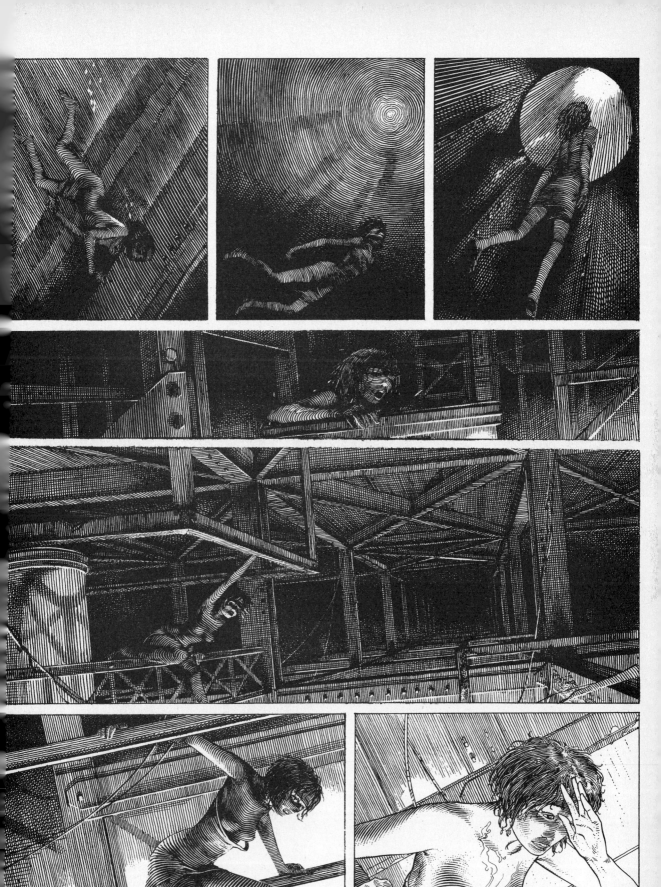

I'VE CONCLUDED THAT OUR EARTH IS LIKE A BALL THAT NEVER STOPS ROTATING, A BALL SO HUGE THAT IT TAKES 100 PERIODS FOR IT TO COMPLETE A FULL TURN. WE ARE CONDEMNED TO WALK AT THE BOTTOM OF THE SPHERE UNTIL THE END OF OUR DAYS. I DON'T THINK THAT--

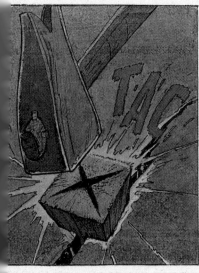

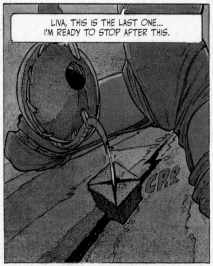

LIVA, THIS IS THE LAST ONE... I'M READY TO STOP AFTER THIS.

WHAT ABOUT TOMORROW? ARE YOU SURE YOU STILL WANT TO DO IT?

OF COURSE. YOU KNOW THAT I WOULDN'T GIVE UP NOW!

I'VE BEEN WAITING FOR THE RAY OF LIGHT TO COINCIDE WITH MY CYCLE FOR SUCH A LONG TIME...

IT'S ALL RIGHT, LIVA... YOU CAN GO NOW.

YOU KNOW, THIS IS ONE OF MY GREATEST DREAMS... IT MUST BE LOVELY TO CREATE A NEW LITTLE GAMMA.

EVEN IF IT'S ONE OF THE THINGS I'M MOST AFRAID OF...

...TO BE INSEMINATED BY THE LIGAM...

AFRAID OF THAT GIANT SLUG?

TO THINK THAT ALL THIS WORK IS BASED ON VAGUE PREDICTIONS... IF YOU'RE WRONG, JENNI, YOU'LL HAVE TO FACE THE ENTIRE COMMUNITY AND GIVE THEM SOME KIND OF EXPLANATION...

IT'S A GAMBLE, BUT I HAD TO SPEAK UP. I DON'T THINK WE'LL EVER REGRET IT.

BUT YOU STILL MUST HAVE AT LEAST SOME IDEA OF *WHAT* WE'LL FIND IN THE DEPTHS OF THAT TUNNEL!

MY GUESS IS THAT IT WILL BE SOME FORM OF *ENERGY*, BUT I HAVE NO IDEA WHAT KIND. MAYBE LIGHT, MAYBE FOOD...

I'D PREFER LIGHT. EVERYTHING'S SO BEAUTIFUL WHEN IT'S ILLUMINATED.

THEN YOU'RE LUCKY. YOU'RE IN FOR A TREAT TOMORROW.

THE NEXT MORNING, AT DAWN...

NELLE, THE TIME HAS COME.

YOUR PARTNER IS READY, NELLE. DO YOU REMEMBER THE PROTOCOL YOU HAVE TO FOLLOW?

YES, OF COURSE. THE WORST PART WILL BE WHEN I HAVE TO *KISS* THAT GIANT SLUG.

BUT I KNOW I *HAVE TO* DO IT IF I DON'T WANT TO END UP LIKE LURISSE.

QUIET, NELLE! YOU KNOW YOU AREN'T SUPPOSED TO TALK ABOUT THAT.

THERE!

THE LIGHT HAS STRUCK THE BLUE ROCK. *HURRY UP!*

DON'T WORRY. ALL WILL BE WELL.

WE'LL WAIT FOR YOU HERE. GOOD LUCK, NELLE!

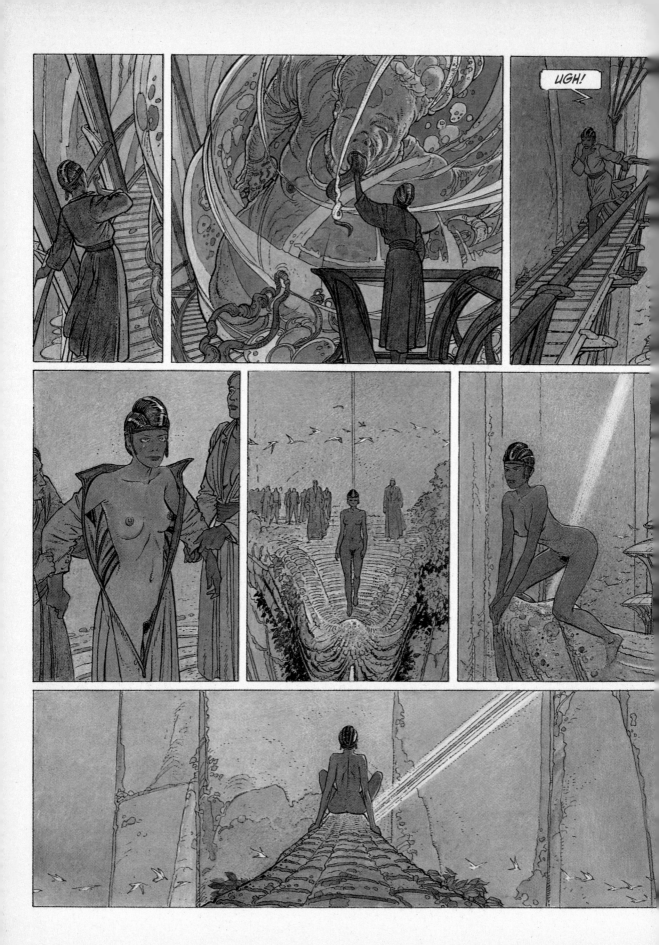

MEANWHILE, ON A SMALL PLANET MANY LIGHT YEARS AWAY...

WHAT MORE DO YOU WANT, ORION? WE HAVE EVERYTHING WE NEED HERE. WE COULD STAY HERE FOR ETERNITY.

EVERYTHING, EXCEPT WHAT I WANT MOST: ACTION... THE CONQUEST OF WOMEN!

YESTERDAY I READ IN THE GRAND ENCYCLOPEDIA THAT WE'RE LOCATED CLOSE TO A GROUP OF SEVEN PLANETS CALLED *"THE HOLLOW GROUNDS."*

IS THAT SO?... WHAT'S ON YOUR MIND, ORION...?

I'LL SKIP THE DESCRIPTION OF THE FIRST FOUR PLANETS AND GO STRAIGHT TO ZARA...THE ONE THAT INTERESTS ME *MOST*...

"ZARA, THE FIFTH PLANET, IS COMPOSED OF TWO CONCENTRIC LAYERS THAT ARE INDEPENDENT OF EACH OTHER. THE OUTER LAYER REVOLVES CONTINUOUSLY. THE INNER ONE, HOWEVER, SEEMS TO STAY FIXED. THE FIRST LAYER IS COVERED BY VEGETATION AND TRANSLUCENT ROCKS, SOME OF THEM AS PURE AS CRYSTAL."

"THE DESCRIPTIONS OF THEIR SAPPHIC PRACTICES ARE SO FANCIFUL THAT WE CAN'T REALLY TAKE THEM SERIOUSLY. HOWEVER, THE HYPOTHESIS THAT THIS SOCIETY HAS REMAINED AS IT IS UNTIL NOW DUE TO ITS PROTECTIVE OUTER LAYER MAY WELL BE TRUE."

AND I HAVEN'T MENTIONED THE BEST PART, "...SOME EXPLORERS TELL US THAT THROUGH THESE CRYSTAL ROCKS THEY HAVE OBSERVED A PEACEFUL CIVILIZATION MADE UP ENTIRELY OF WOMEN... THEY HAVE EVOLVED THERE IN COMPLETE ISOLATION WITHOUT EVER COMING IN CONTACT WITH THE REST OF THE WORLD.

SO, WHAT DO YOU SAY? DOESN'T THIS LOOK LIKE IT MIGHT QUENCH OUR THIRST FOR CONQUEST?

THE VOYAGE WOULD BE REASONABLY SHORT.

A PLANET INHABITED ENTIRELY BY WOMEN... IT'S INCREDIBLE!

WE'RE AGREED, THEN. WE'RE OFF TO *ZARA!*

MEANWHILE...

YOU SEE, NELLE, EVERYTHING TURNED OUT FOR THE BEST.

YES! IT REALLY DID GO WELL!

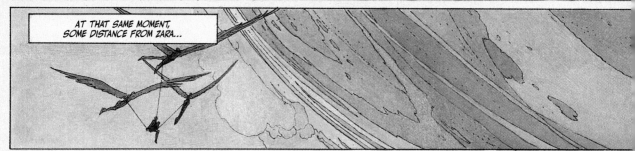

AT THAT SAME MOMENT, SOME DISTANCE FROM ZARA...

ON THE INTERIOR OF THE PLANET ZARA, TWO PARALLEL VERTICAL WORLDS STRETCH OUT AS FAR AS THE EYE CAN SEE. TO THE LEFT IS THE VILLAGE OF THE GAMMAS, EMBEDDED IN THE VERTICAL WALL OF ROCK, AND MUCH HIGHER ABOVE IT ARE THEIR CULTIVATED FIELDS. ACROSS FROM THE VILLAGE IS THE WALL THAT HOLDS THE VAST OPEN SPACES, ITS FERTILE PLAINS, ITS ARID DESERTS, ITS FORESTS OF ROOTS AND ITS CRYSTAL ROCKS.

BETWEEN THE TWO WALLS, GIANT THRESHERS PROCESS RIPE STALKS OF WHEAT.

NELLE, MOVE IT MORE TO THE RIGHT!

BECAUSE THE WHEAT FIELDS ARE ON A VERTICAL AXIS, THE MACHINERY'S WHEELS TURN SMOOTHLY, PROVIDING THE MOMENTUM FOR ITS COMPLICATED MECHANISM.

THE BAG WILL BE FULL SOON.

I'D BETTER EMPTY IT INTO A STORAGE BIN.

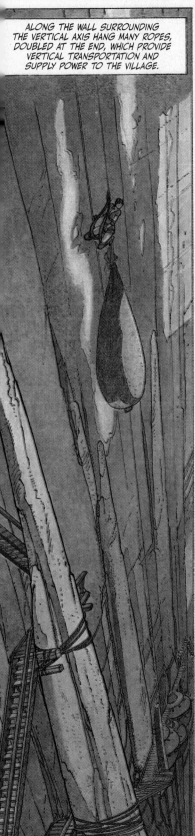

ALONG THE WALL SURROUNDING THE VERTICAL AXIS HANG MANY ROPES, DOUBLED AT THE END, WHICH PROVIDE VERTICAL TRANSPORTATION AND SUPPLY POWER TO THE VILLAGE.

AAH!

?

GINA AND FANETTE! WHAT ARE YOU *DOING* THERE?

OH, IT'S YOU, NELLE! WELL - WE - UH...

WE WERE JUST MAKING SURE THAT OUR SUPPLIES HADN'T BEEN ATTACKED. IF THE VICHNOUS EVER GOT AT THEM, THEY COULD CAUSE A LOT OF DAMAGE!

THE VICHNOUS? BUT THEY HAVEN'T BEEN AROUND FOR CYCLES!

YOU NEVER KNOW. WE JUST WANTED TO MAKE CERTAIN.

VICHNOUS INDEED! A LIKELY STORY!

IN THE EVENING... THE GAMMAS SIT ON THEIR ROPES AND WAIT FOR LIVA TO PROJECT HER IMAGES.

I'M ALMOST READY.

HEY, NELLE!

NELLE! DO YOU KNOW WHICH DREAM LIVA IS PROJECTING TONIGHT?

I HAVE NO IDEA, JENNI. IT'S ALWAYS HARD TO TELL WHAT SHE'S THINKING.

EVEN THOUGH YOU'RE HER COMPANION? I ASSUMED SHE CONFIDED IN YOU, AT LEAST.

NO, SHE'S A VERY PRIVATE PERSON.

THE ONLY TIME SHE REALLY COMMUNICATES IS WHEN SHE PROJECTS HER DREAMS, AND THEN SHE TRANSMITS IMAGES BETTER THAN ANYONE ELSE...

WATCH... SHE'S ABOUT TO START!

...THOSE ARE... THOSE ARE... GAMMAS WITH WINGS...

...THEY FLY VERY GENTLY... WITHOUT A SOUND...

...IN A DENSE FOREST... A SWEET SMELL OF FLOWERS...

...AN OPEN CLEARING... LOTS OF LIGHT...

...A FRESH BREEZE IS BLOWING...

...THEY ARE MOVING TOWARD ONE OF THE TALLEST PLANTS...

...THIS PLANT...

HELP!

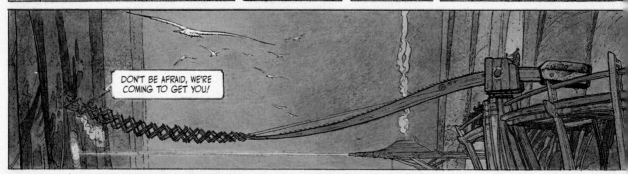

THAT'S IT! SHE'S *SAVED!*

THE NEXT DAY...

I HEARD THAT HER NAME IS OLIVE.

SHE TOLD SOMEONE THAT SHE CAME FROM ANOTHER PLANET. SHE WAS BROUGHT HERE BY FLITTERS...

FLITTERS... I DIDN'T KNOW THEY STILL EXISTED...

SHE FOUND HER WAY THROUGH THE ROCKS, JUST LIKE THE FLITTERS USED TO DO MANY CYCLES AGO, WHEN THEY RAIDED OUR SUPPLIES.

WHAT'S IT LIKE IN HER WORLD?

SHE'LL TELL US THIS EVENING.

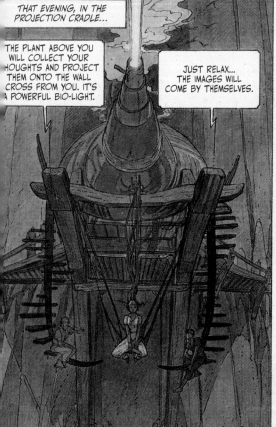

THAT EVENING, IN THE PROJECTION CRADLE...

THE PLANT ABOVE YOU WILL COLLECT YOUR THOUGHTS AND PROJECT THEM ONTO THE WALL ACROSS FROM YOU. IT'S A POWERFUL BIO-LIGHT.

JUST RELAX... THE IMAGES WILL COME BY THEMSELVES.

...MY PLANET IS...IS...ABOUT THREE CYCLES AWAY...AS THE FLITTERS FLY... WE...WE LIVE ON ITS INTERIOR SURFACE...

...SINCE THE SURFACE IS CONSTANTLY TURNING, WE ARE FORCED TO MOVE ALL THE TIME...

...SO AS TO ALWAYS LIVE IN THE LOWEST PART.

IT'S DIFFICULT TO IMAGINE A HORIZONTAL WORLD!

YOU CAN WALK ALONG THE SHORE ALL DAY? IT MUST BE WONDERFUL TO BATHE WHENEVER YOU WANT.

NO, ONLY IN THE EVENING... WHEN OUR TRIBE STOPS TO REST, EVERYONE GOES INTO THE WATER. IT'S THE BEST TIME OF THE DAY...

LOOK! THOSE DON'T LOOK LIKE EITHER GAMMAS OR FLITTERS...

IT'S TRUE, THEY LOOK VERY DIFFERENT FROM US!

WHAT'S THAT BELOW THEIR STOMACHS? IT SEEMS LIKE SOME KIND OF VINE.

WHAT'S THAT THING FOR?

YOU WOULDN'T KNOW ABOUT THAT, WITH NO ME HERE. I'LL SHOW YOU.

AMAZING!

HUMAN BEINGS WITH VINES... HOW ASTONISHING!

NOTHING LIKE THE LIGAM, THAT BIG SLUG!

IT'S INCREDIBLE! WHAT A WORLD!

IT MUST BE WONDERFUL TO BE VINED BY ONE OF THOSE.

IT WOULD BE FANTASTIC IF WE COULD HAVE THIS NEW KIND OF INSEMINATOR IN OUR WORLD.

OLIVE, DO YOU THINK IT MIGHT BE POSSIBLE FOR YOU TO BRING BACK ONE OF THOSE CREATURES YOU SHOWED US?

THEY'D NEVER AGREE TO FOLLOW ME. THEY'RE TOO AFRAID TO STOP WALKING...

WE'LL TELL THEM THAT THEY WOULDN'T BE FORCED TO WALK ANYMORE... THEY'D BE HAPPY HERE...LOOK AT HOW GOOD THE LIGAM HAS IT!

BUT WHY CHANGE ANYTHING? HOW WOULD THOSE FREAKS OF NATURE BENEFIT US?

...REMEMBER WHAT THE ELDER ONES USED TO SAY...

...CREATURES LIKE THOSE USED TO COME TO THE VILLAGE ONCE IN A WHILE AND THERE WOULD ALWAYS BE GREAT REJOICING AND FESTIVITIES THAT LASTED MANY DAYS. THE ELDER ONES STILL SPEAK FONDLY OF THOSE CELEBRATIONS.

I REMEMBER... I WAS STILL SO YOUNG THEN...

WHAT HAPPENED TO THEM? WHY AREN'T THEY STILL LIVING AMONG YOU?

WE SHOULD LOOK FOR MORE OF THEM.

THEY'VE GONE CRAZY...

OLIVE, WOULD YOU HELP US?

WE'LL PREPARE AN EXPEDITION!

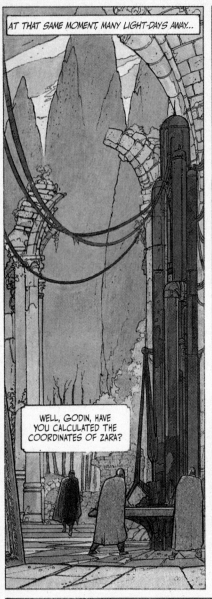

AT THAT SAME MOMENT, MANY LIGHT-DAYS AWAY...

WELL, GODIN, HAVE YOU CALCULATED THE COORDINATES OF ZARA?

YES, I'M ALMOST DONE...WE'LL SOON BE ABLE TO REMATERIALIZE NEAR ZARA.

I'D LIKE TO ESTABLISH OUR NEW HEADQUARTERS THERE. ZARA'S OUTER LAYER WOULD BE AN EFFECTIVE NATURAL DEFENSE STRUCTURE.

HOW DO I LOOK IN THESE?

YOU'RE PERFECT AS ALWAYS, ORION. I CAN ALREADY PICTURE THE EXPRESSIONS ON THEIR FACES WHEN THEY SEE US.

I MUST SAY THAT I LIKE THE IDEA OF EXCHANGING OUR USUAL ATTIRE FOR MEDIEVAL GARMENTS AND ARMOR...

YES, THEY'RE CERTAINLY MORE ATTRACTIVE!

AND WHAT'S MORE, I DON'T RELISH THE THOUGHT OF DISINTEGRATING THE GAMMAS WITH OUR REGULAR WEAPONS. OH, THE UNSPEAKABLE PLEASURE OF FEELING THE BLADE PENETRATE FLESH... THE CRIES... WARM BLOOD FLOWING...

OLIVE, WOULD COME TO MY ROOM? I'D LIKE TO TALK TO YOU...

YES? WHAT'S THE MATTER?

SHHH. I'LL TELL YOU WHEN WE'RE ALONE...

?

COULD YOU TELL ME WHAT YOU KNOW ABOUT THOSE STRANGE CREATURES YOU SHOWED US YESTERDAY? YOU MUST TELL ME EVERYTHING!

BUT I TOLD YOU ALL LAST NIGHT...

YES, BUT I WANT TO KNOW MORE. I'D LIKE YOU TO EXPLAIN WHAT IT FEELS LIKE TO HAVE ONE OF THOSE VINES INSIDE YOU...

AFTERWARDS, IF YOU WANT, I'LL SHOW YOU WHAT WE DO HERE, AMONG OURSELVES.

THANKS... THE OTHERS HAVE ALREADY SHOWN ME...

ALL RIGHT. THEN TELL ME...

WE'RE READY. YOU'LL DESCEND THROUGH THE WORLD IN-BETWEEN UNTIL YOU COME TO A GAP LARGE ENOUGH FOR YOU TO PASS THROUGH TO THE OUTER LAYER.

FROM THERE WE'LL SEARCH FOR THE FLITTERS AND ASK THEM TO TAKE US TO OLIVE'S PLANET.

DON'T FORGET YOUR CURRENCY. HERE'S A BAG OF BALIK. THEY LOVE THAT.

BUT DON'T TRUST THOSE FLITTERS. THEY MAY NOT HAVE FORGOTTEN THAT WE CHASED THEM AWAY A LONG TIME AGO. THOSE BEASTS HAVE GOOD MEMORIES.

GOOD LUCK!

DON'T TAKE ANY CHANCES!

PICK THE BEST-LOOKING ONES!

OFF THEY GO!

HAVE A SAFE TRIP!

GOODBYE, OLIVE!

WE'VE BEEN PREPARING FOR THIS EXPEDITION FOR SO LONG.

IT'S TIME WE FOUND OUT WHAT WAS DOWN THERE, AT THE END OF THE WORLD IN-BETWEEN.

WE'VE MADE IT - WE'RE OUT OF THE ROOTS! NOW WE JUST HAVE TO STOP.

YES, LIVA'S STILL WAITING UP THERE.

!

I CAN'T FIND ANYWHERE TO ANCHOR IT ON THE WALL.

THE SURFACE IS TOO SMOOTH.

WE'RE DESCENDING TOO FAST!

THIS EXPEDITION WORRIES ME. NELLE AND LIVA HAVE NO REAL EXPERIENCE...AND WHY DID THEY TAKE OLIVE WITH THEM? SHE KNOWS NOTHING ABOUT OUR WORLD.

THAT'S TRUE. BUT SHE KNOWS ABOUT MEN AND OTHER PLANETS - THAT'S A GREAT ADVANTAGE.

COME AND HELP ME!

I CAN'T MOVE THIS ROCK.

PUSH!

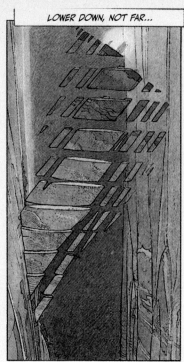

LOWER DOWN, NOT FAR...

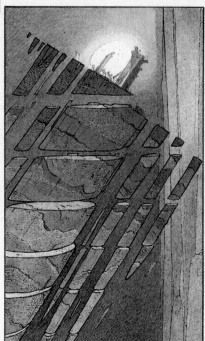

ZARA! *FINALLY!*

YOU SHOULD HAVE TAKEN MORE CARE. WE'RE NOT ON LEVEL GROUND.

TRAVELING BY DEMATERIALIZATION IS DIFFICULT, SOMETHING ALWAYS GOES WRONG. WERE OUR COORDINATES ACCURATE, GODIN?

WE LANDED BETWEEN TWO ROCK WALLS. THAT COINCIDES WITH MY CALCULATIONS.

I CAN'T WAIT TO FIND OUT IF THIS PLANET IS ACTUALLY AS THE ENCYCLOPEDIA DESCRIBED IT. CAN YOU DETECT THE PRESENCE OF HUMANS?

IN A FEW MINUTES--THE IMAGES ARE FORMING. ... HERE THEY ARE. YES. WITHOUT A DOUBT.

WE'RE VERY CLOSE TO ONE OR TWO LIVING BEINGS, PROBABLY THOSE FAMOUS GAMMAS... I THINK I SEE ANOTHER RIGHT BELOW THEM. AND MUCH HIGHER UP THERE'S A CLUSTER OF THEM.

THAT'S WHERE THE VILLAGE MUST BE, ON THE OPPOSITE WALL.

WELL, THIS LOOKS VERY PROMISING.

HEY, *LOOK!* THE OPPOSITE WALL IS MOVING. IT SEEMS TO BE DESCENDING.

MAYBE THIS ONE IS RISING.

THAT'S PERFECT! WE'RE GETTING CLOSER TO THOSE CREATURES AND THEIR VILLAGE.

WE CAN JUST SIT BACK AND WAIT.

THEY'RE GETTING FURTHER AWAY FROM ME. I MIGHT BE ABLE TO CATCH UP TO THEM WITH A ROPE.

I HOPE IT'S LONG ENOUGH.

I GUESS THEY COULDN'T STOP.

FINISHED! I'VE RUN OUT OF ROPE.

I HAVE TO REACH THE VILLAGE WALL!

THE ROCK IS VERY SOFT. I'LL MAKE THIS LEDGE A LITTLE WIDER.

THAT'S MUCH MORE COMFORTABLE. THIS ROCK FORMATION IS VERY ODD; I'VE NEVER SEEN ONE LIKE IT.

NOT EVEN THE SLIGHTEST CRACK. I'M STARTING TO GET WORRIED...

WE MUST BE ABLE TO DO SOMETHING. THERE! HURRY, OLIVE, HELP ME!

DONE! WE'RE ALREADY RISING.

MEANWHILE...

LOOK! SOMETHING IS MOVING UP THERE.

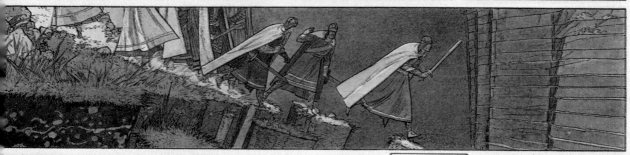

IN THE TUNNEL...

ALL THIS DUST!

A WARM BREEZE... AND THAT STRANGE LUMINESCENCE... IT LOOKS LIKE...

WHITE LIGHT!

IT'S INCREDIBLE! WE'VE BEEN SEARCHING FOR THIS LIGHT FOR HUNDREDS OF CYCLES...

WE'LL GET THE MOBILE MIRROR AND ILLUMINATE THE WHOLE VILLAGE.

A LITTLE MORE TO THE RIGHT... PERFECT! THIS ANGLE IS IDEAL...

THIS LIGHT IS SO SOFT... LIKE A GENTLE CARESS...

TO BE BATHED IN LIGHT... I'VE NEVER FELT ANYTHING LIKE THIS...

MEANWHILE, FAR BELOW...

I CAN'T HEAR ANYTHING ELSE...

WAIT! LISTEN!

MEN! GET AWAY!

POOR THING... SHE'S GONE...

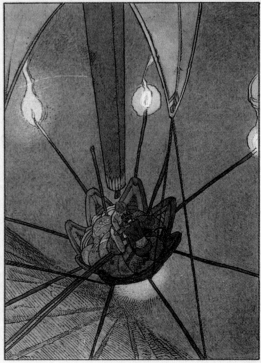

SHE WAS TRYING TO WARN US. THERE MUST BE MEN AROUND HERE...

MEN! BUT WHY DO YOU THINK THEY'D BE DANGEROUS?

YOU COULDN'T UNDERSTAND.

ANYWAY, WE CAN'T JUST STAY HERE. WE HAVE TO GO BACK AND FIND OUT WHAT HAPPENED TO HER!

WE'RE TAKING A GREAT RISK. WE'D HAVE TO PASS THE SPOT WHERE THE MEN ATTACKED LIVA... THEY MUST STILL BE AROUND THERE.

IF THAT'S TRUE, ALL THE OTHER GAMMAS ARE IN DANGER... WE DON'T HAVE A MOMENT TO LOSE!

YOU'RE RIGHT... WE MUST REACH THE VILLAGE BEFORE THE MEN GET THERE.

HOW WILL WE DO THAT?

I'LL UNHOOK ONE OF THE PETALS.

DONE! LOOSEN THE ROPES AND RAISE THE HOOKS.

THERE! NOW WE'LL LET THE PETAL GO UNTIL IT HOOKS ONTO SOMETHING.

A LITTLE LATER...

GREAT! IT STOPPED. WE CAN GO.

JUST IN TIME. WE ALMOST USED ALL OF OUR ROPE.

I HOPE WE'LL GET THERE IN TIME.

THAT STRANGE ROCK WASN'T THERE WHEN WE CAME DOWN... WE MUST BE NEAR THE BOTTOM.

THAT LITTLE ONE JUMPED TO HER DEATH JUST WHEN WE WERE STARTING TO HAVE SOME FUN.

CALM DOWN, ORION. THERE ARE MORE GAMMAS AROUND... IT WON'T BE LONG BEFORE WE REACH THEIR VILLAGE.

BE CAREFUL... THEY MUST BE UP THERE.

ORION... LOOK AT THE SCREEN! TWO OF THEM ARE RIGHT BELOW US, LESS THAN THREE LENGTHS AWAY.

MARVELOUS! ALL WE HAVE TO DO IS GRAB THEM.

DID YOU HEAR THAT?

HOW CAN WE REACH THEM?

THEY HAVE TO COME THIS WAY TO RETURN TO THEIR VILLAGE.

THEY'RE SO CLOSE... RIGHT BELOW US, IN THE SHADOWS. I CAN SENSE THEM THERE...

PATIENCE, ORION, PATIENCE...

SHHHH...

LATER...

WE'RE BACK IN THE ROOT FOREST... WE'RE NOT FAR FROM THE VILLAGE...

WE HAVE TO FIND A WAY TO GET THERE BEFORE THEM!

THEY'RE WATCHING US. WE HAVE TO MOVE *QUICKLY!*

I THINK I HAVE AN IDEA...

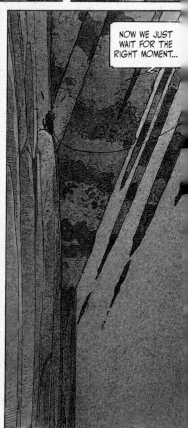

NOW WE JUST WAIT FOR THE RIGHT MOMENT...

OOK! WE'VE REACHED THE LONGER ROPES.

NOW!

GOT IT! I'VE GOT ONE.

THERE THEY ARE! THEY'RE BELOW US... *QUICK*, HAND ME MY CROSSBOW!

THERE'S A GOOD DISTANCE BETWEEN THE TWO WALLS. THEY WON'T BE ABLE TO REACH US.

THIS IS GREAT. I'M GOING TO PIN THEM TO THE ROCK!

CLIC

HELL! THIS THING ISN'T CHARGED! I CAN'T GET USED TO THESE ARCHAIC WEAPONS...

HURRY, THE GAMMAS ARE LEAVING US BEHIND...

TOO LATE... THEY'RE OUT OF MY RANGE...

TO MISS SUCH AN EASY TARGET!

HERE'S THE MIRROR INSTALLATION.

LOOK! NELLE AND OLIVE! THEY'RE BACK!

OOH! BELOW THEM... SOME OF THOSE CREATURES WITH VINES...

THEY'VE RETURNED!

LET'S GO WELCOME THEM!

RUN! RUN FAST! THEY'RE KILLERS!

RUN? RUN WHERE?

THE BASKETS HAVE GONE BACK UP...

QUICK! THEY'VE KILLED LIVA!

"THE TUNNEL...IT'S OUR ONLY HOPE!"

FIRST, THOSE WHO ESCAPED INTO THE TUNNEL...

A PARALLEL TUNNEL! THIS WAY!

THEY'RE RIGHT BEHIND US. HURRY!

THEY MUST HAVE GONE THIS WAY. THEY WON'T BE ABLE TO ESCAPE.

THIS EXIT IS THE CLOSEST. I HOPE THE ROPES AND BASKETS ARE THERE.

WE'RE TRAPPED!

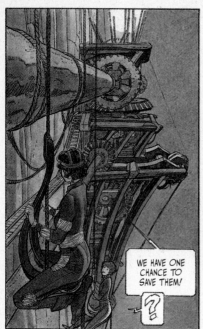

WE HAVE ONE CHANCE TO SAVE THEM!

I THINK THIS WILL WORK. THE ROPES ARE DIRECTLY ABOVE THEM.

THOSE KILLERS HAVEN'T WON YET!

THE ROPES!

OH HELL! THEY'RE GETTING AWAY *AGAIN*.

PERFECT! THEY'VE GONE DOWN TO THE LOWER BALCONY.

THEY'RE STUCK DOWN THERE. THEY HAVE NOWHERE TO RUN. THEY'RE ALL OURS.

WHAT? GO DOWN ON THOSE ROPES? *NEVER!*

WE CAN'T VERY WELL LET THEM GO.

COME ON! FOLLOW ME!

IT'S WORKING!

WHAT'S HAPPENING? WE'RE *CLIMBING.*

UP THERE! ABOVE US... THEY'RE RAISING THE ROPES.

WE MUST GET DOWN. FAST.

THIS IS INSANITY!

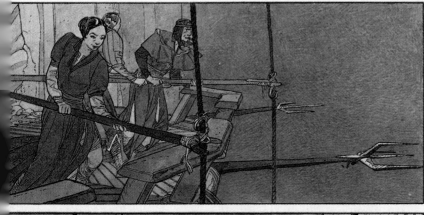

TRUST ME, ORION. IF WE EVER GET OUT OF HERE, YOUR FUTURE WON'T BE *ENVIABLE!*

SO, ORION, WHAT DO YOU WANT TO DO NOW?

THAT WAS A BRILLIANT IDEA: LEAVE BEHIND OUR TRUSTED WEAPONS TO ATTACK YOUNG, DEFENSELESS WOMEN...

WE CAN'T JUST LEAVE THEM THERE. WE'LL LOSE THEM IN THE VOID.

LET'S BRING THEM BACK UP. ONCE WE DISARM THEM, WE'LL BE ABLE TO STUDY THEM ONE BY ONE IN THE EXAMINATION CHAMBER.

LATER...

THIS LOOKS JUST LIKE THOSE IMAGES OLIVE PROJECTED ON OUR WALL.

WHAT A CURIOUS PHENOMENON.

HOW UNIQUE...AND INTERESTING!

NOW THE ELDER ONES WILL MEET AND DECIDE WHAT TO DO WITH THEM.

TOO BAD. I WOULD LOVE TO KNOW WHAT YOU'RE GOING TO DO TO THEM.

LATER...

WE'VE AGREED, INSTEAD OF WASTING THEM ALL AT ONCE, WE'LL USE ONE EVERY THREE MONTHS... THAT WAY OUR FESTIVITIES WILL LAST FOR ONE ENTIRE CYCLE.

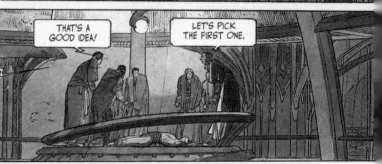

THAT'S A GOOD IDEA!

LET'S PICK THE FIRST ONE.

THEY'RE DISPLAYED TO THEIR FULLEST ADVANTAGE.

WE HAVE SOME VERY FINE-LOOKING SPECIMENS.

I HAVEN'T SEEN SUCH A SPECTACU-LAR SIGHT IN A LONG TIME.

GREAT!

IF WE BEGIN WITH THE UGLIEST, WE'D SAVE THE BEST FOR LAST.

THE VIEW ALONE IS REJUVENATING ME BY SEVERAL CYCLES.

THIS ONE SEEMS APPETIZING. HE'LL BE AN EXCELLENT START.

WHAT ABOUT THIS ONE?

WE SHOULD REALLY CONSIDER EVERY ASPECT OF THE SPECIMEN...WITHOUT LETTING OURSELVES BE INFLUENCED BY THE MORE ATTRACTIVE DETAILS.

THEN IT'S AGREED, WE'LL START WITH THE ONE WHO SEEMS TO BE THEIR LEADER.

THIS GRILL HAS BEEN UNUSED FOR SO LONG.

FORTUNATELY, THE ELDER ONES HAVE TAKEN CARE OF IT FOR MANY CYCLES.

DON'T FORGET THE BALMS AND THE SCENTED OILS.

WHO SHALL BEGIN?

I WANT TO GO FIRST!

AAAAHH!

SO! WHAT DID YOU THINK?

IT WAS INCREDIBLE. I'VE NEVER FELT ANYTHING LIKE IT!

OLIVE, IS SOMETHING WRONG?

I... I'M NOT QUITE USED TO YOUR *CUSTOMS*.

IN OUR WORLD, PEOPLE HAVE INTERCOURSE VERY DISCREETLY... OUR WORLD IS VERY DIFFERENT FROM YOURS.

IT CERTAINLY IS... AND IT'S PROBABLY EVEN MORE DIFFERENT THAN YOU THINK.

COME WITH ME TO THE OBSERVATION CHAMBER - I'LL TRY TO EXPLAIN A FEW THINGS.

OUR LIFE HERE WAS ONCE VERY DIFFICULT... AS IT IS NOW ON YOUR PLANET. ALL OF OUR ENERGIES WERE FOCUSED ON SURVIVING IN A WORLD FOR WHICH WE WEREN'T SUITED.

IMAGINE HOW PRECARIOUS OUR LIFE WAS - WE HAD DIFFICULTY COMMUNICATING WITH EACH OTHER FROM OUR UNDERGROUND SHELTERS. WE WERE ALWAYS AFRAID OF FALLING INTO THE VOID AND WERE PREYED UPON BY VINDICTIVE AND EVIL HUNTERS.

BUT HOW DID YOU MANAGE TO SURVIVE FOR SO LONG?

DO YOU SEE THOSE INSECTS OVER THERE? THEY'RE CALLED ZARANITES. A GAMMA HAD THE BRILLIANT IDEA OF STUDYING THEM CLOSELY.

I KNOW THEM. WE HAVE THEM IN OUR WORLD, TOO. THEY'RE UGLY SCAVENGERS.

NO, NOT AT ALL! THEY'VE ADAPTED MARVELOUSLY TO THEIR ENVIRONMENT. SEE HOW SWIFTLY THEY MOVE AROUND ON THE WEBS THEY SPIN?

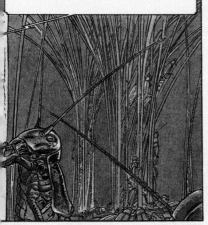

LOOK AT THEIR NESTS - THEY USE THESE SMALL, LOCAL PLANTS TO BUILD GRACEFUL, FLEXIBLE STRUCTURES. THEY TAUGHT US HOW TO BUILD OUR HOUSES.

AND WATCH THOSE, OVER THERE. THAT WEB THEY'RE SPINNING WILL CAPTURE A MALE.

YES, I KNOW WHAT THEY DO TO THOSE POOR MALES WHEN THEY MATE.

WE STUDIED THEM FOR A LONG TIME IN AN ATTEMPT TO UNDERSTAND HOW WE COULD ACHIEVE A SIMILAR SYMBIOSIS BETWEEN OUR WAY OF LIFE AND OUR PLANET.

SURELY YOU DON'T MIMIC ALL OF THEIR BEHAVIORS?!

OF COURSE! TO ACHIEVE THE BALANCE WE WERE LOOKING FOR, WE HAD TO ADOPT THEIR CUSTOMS WITHOUT EXCEPTION. DO YOU UNDERSTAND?

DON'T WORRY, THEY DON'T FEEL *ANYTHING*. COME AND HAVE A LOOK...

MUCH LATER...

THE SECOND PHASE IS ABOUT TO BEGIN!

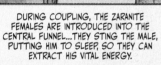

DURING COUPLING, THE ZARANITE FEMALES ARE INTRODUCED INTO THE CENTRAL FUNNEL...THEY STING THE MALE, PUTTING HIM TO SLEEP, SO THEY CAN EXTRACT HIS VITAL ENERGY.

...SOON HE'LL COLLAPSE LIKE AN EMPTY GRAIN SACK....

THE ENERGY WILL BE STORED IN OUR ZARANITE HIVES AND WILL REGENERATE OUR OLD LIGAM... WE WASTE NOTHING.

AND TO THINK THAT I ALMOST BROUGHT THE MEN FROM MY PLANET HERE!

THE END

122

CHAPTER 1

EPOCH 139, 33RD CYCLE, 13TH PERIOD

TODAY I'VE DECIDED TO START KEEPING
A JOURNAL AGAIN. I LEFT BEHIND THE FIRST
ONE IN MY NATIVE LAND. AFTER A SEEMINGLY
ENDLESS VOYAGE I WAS SHIPWRECKED
ON NOGEGON, THE SECOND PLANET IN
THE HOLLOW GROUNDS SYSTEM. WHAT'S
MOST SURPRISING HERE IS THE ALMOST
COMPLETE ABSENCE OF GRAVITY. IT'S 32
TIMES INFERIOR TO GRAVITY ON ZARA.
WITH ONE JUMP I CAN CROSS A DISTANCE
OF 100 FEET. I'VE JUMPED AND DANCED
ALL DAY LONG. I'M VERY LIGHT.

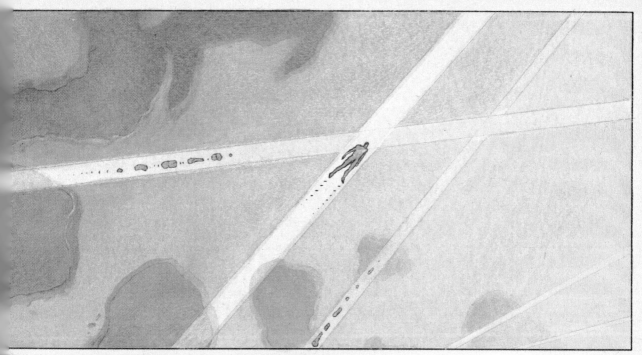

I'VE ALWAYS HATED REJECTS... THEIR CHRONIC ASYMMETRY DISGUSTS ME...

ODD TO HAVE CHOSEN ME FOR THIS MISSION. I, WHO HARDLY KNOW ANYTHING ABOUT THEM...

IT CAN ONLY BE BECAUSE I'M SO SWIFT AND EFFICIENT ON THE GROUND. LOOKS PROMISING!

NO ONE AT THE JUMP-RECEPTOR.

I SHOULD BE ABLE TO FIND SOMEONE IN THERE.

THAT MUST BE THE ENTRANCE.

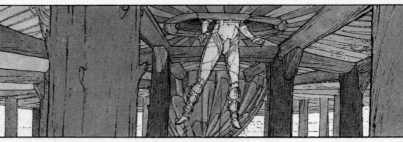

I'M INSPECTOR "S" FROM DRAMARD. I'D LIKE TO ASK THE PERSON IN CHARGE OF THIS SECTOR A FEW QUESTIONS.

PSSSST...
INSPECTOR...

PLEASE, TAKE ME OUT OF HERE! I'LL TELL YOU ALL I KNOW ABOUT THESE PEOPLE.

WHAT A FOOL! THEY MUST HAVE HEARD HER. IF I LEAVE HER HERE SHE'LL BE IN A LOT OF TROUBLE.

GET READY! WE'LL TAKE THEM BY SURPRISE.

HA... A...

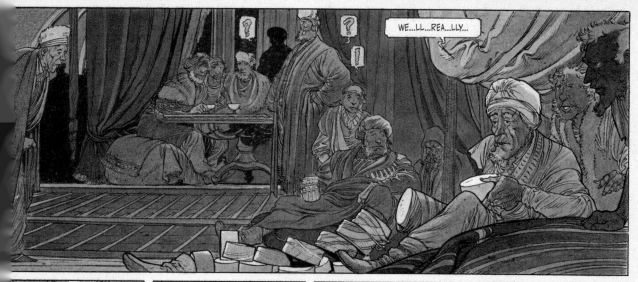

WE...LL...REA...LLY...

JUST...WHEN...
I...WAS...

GO...ING...TO...
TELL...HIM...

UN...

THIS...IN...SPEC...

BE...LIEVE...ABLE...

TOR...IS...CRAZY...

THAT WAS HORRIBLE... WHY DID YOU DO
THAT? THEY TOOK ME IN AND HELPED ME FROM
THE MOMENT I ARRIVED ON NOGEGON...

IT WAS THEM OR US! I SAVED YOUR LIFE.

YOU THINK SO?
THEY SEEMED SO NICE...

OF COURSE I'M RIGHT. *WHO* ARE YOU,
BY THE WAY, AND WHERE DO YOU COME FROM?
YOU'RE OBVIOUSLY A STRANGER HERE.

MY NAME IS NELLE. I COME FROM
THE PLANET ZARA. AND I WANT TO
GO TO DRAMARD.

THAT'S IMPOSSIBLE - THE CITY IS
OFF-LIMITS FOR REJECTS. YOU MUST
HAVE AN ID RING TO GET IN AND YOU
DON'T HAVE ONE.

THAT DOESN'T MATTER.
I'LL GET IN SOMEHOW. I MUST
GET THERE. I'M LOOKING
FOR A FRIEND...

NO... *STAY!*

YOU WON'T GET IN WITHOUT MY HELP, AND I'M WILLING TO HELP YOU IF YOU GIVE ME THE INFORMATION I NEED. A NUMBER OF FOOD SHIPMENTS HAVE DISAPPEARED...

SHIPMENTS?

YES, THEY SHOULD HAVE REBOUNDED OFF HERE AND GONE STRAIGHT TO REUGUER. BUT THEY NEVER GOT THERE. I HAVE REASON TO BELIEVE THAT THEY WERE STOLEN IN THIS SECTOR.

IT'S CERTAINLY POSSIBLE. THEY OFTEN BRING BACK RED PARCELS THAT APPEAR TO CONTAIN A DRUG THAT MAKES THEM TOTALLY PASSIVE.

NO, I'M NOT TALKING ABOUT THOSE PACKAGES. WE WANT THEM TO RECEIVE THE NARCOTICS. I'M TALKING ABOUT SOMETHING ENTIRELY DIFFERENT.

?!

I CAN SEE I'LL HAVE TO TELL YOU EVERYTHING...

...SO THESE REJECTS AREN'T RESPONSIBLE FOR THE DISAPPEARANCES? I'VE GOT TO RESTART MY INVESTIGATION... I'M GOING BACK TO DRAMARD WITH YOU.

HOW ARE WE GOING TO GET THROUGH THE SECURITY SYSTEM?

WHAT...HAP...PENED... MY... POOR... FRIEND?

A...SYM...MET...RICS... GOT...EX...CITED...FOR NO...REASON...AT... ALL...I...DON'T... UN...DER...STAND...

A...SYM...MET...RICS?...THEN.... THERE'S...NO...NEED...TO...WORRY.

AH... GOOD...

AAHHH!

YOU *BITCH!* YOU'LL PAY FOR THAT!

I'M GOING TO *REPORT* YOU TO THE ILLEGAL IMMIGRATION DEPARTMENT. COME HERE!

NO WAY! I WON'T LET YOU TAKE ADVANTAGE OF ME! GOOD-BYE...

NO! *COME BACK!* THE HELICUTTER...

SHE ENTERED THE OTHER RECEPTOR.

OH WELL, SHE'LL GET WHAT SHE DESERVES...

I GOT RID OF HIM AT LAST, THOUGH I MUST ADMIT HE WAS QUITE USEFUL.

EXCUSE ME. I'M LOOKING FOR A FRIEND. CAN YOU TELL ME WHO WOULD BE ABLE TO HELP ME FIND HER?

YOU SHOULD SEE THE SYMMETRY KEEPER FOR THIS DISTRICT. HE'S IN THE MIDDLE BUILDING.

?!

THIS MUST BE IT.

WHICH DISTRICT ARE YOU FROM?

WELL...NONE QUITE YET. I'VE JUST ARRIVED AND I'M LOOKING FOR A FRIEND. SHE'S A FOREIGNER ON NOGEGON. HER NAME IS OLIVE.

I'M SORRY, I'VE NEVER COME ACROSS THAT NAME. SHE CERTAINLY HASN'T LIVED AROUND HERE. YOU SHOULD VISIT THE SYMMETRY KEEPERS FOR THE OTHER DISTRICTS. AND DON'T FORGET TO SIGN UP AS SOON AS POSSIBLE AND DECLARE ALL YOUR SYMMETRICAL ACTIVITIES!

WELL...YES, OF COURSE...

?

A CHECKPOINT! IT'S TOO LATE TO TURN BACK NOW...

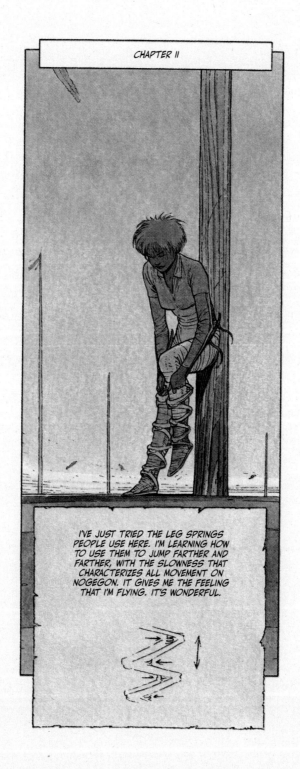

I'VE JUST TRIED THE LEG SPRINGS PEOPLE USE HERE. I'M LEARNING HOW TO USE THEM TO JUMP FARTHER AND FARTHER, WITH THE SLOWNESS THAT CHARACTERIZES ALL MOVEMENT ON NOGEGON. IT GIVES ME THE FEELING THAT I'M FLYING. IT'S WONDERFUL.

FINDING OLIVE IN THIS STRANGE CITY WILL BE MUCH HARDER THAN I THOUGHT.

NO!

SHE CAME HERE SOME TIME AGO. SINCE IT'S A MATTER OF PUBLIC RECORD, I'M FREE TO TELL YOU ALL I KNOW.

WHERE IS SHE NOW?

NO, NEVER HEARD OF HER.

YES... I THINK I REMEMBER SOMETHING. WAIT A MOMENT, PLEASE...

OH, THEN YOU DON'T KNOW? SHE KILLED HERSELF ALMOST A CYCLE AGO...

OH *NOOO!* IT *CAN'T* BE TRUE!

SHE WAS DEPRESSED. SHE HAD NEVER GOTTEN USED TO OUR LIFESTYLE. SHE THREW HERSELF INTO THE OUTSIDE VOID... SHE LIVED WITH A SCULPTRACER FOR A LONG TIME, IN THE 44TH DISTRICT.

YOU'RE LUCKY THAT I STILL HAD THESE OLD FILES AROUND. I SHOULD HAVE SENT EVERYTHING OFF TO THE CHIEF SYMMETRY KEEPER. HE'S THE ONE WHO'LL VERIFY THE COMPLETE RECORD ONE LAST TIME.

BUT HE STILL HASN'T SENT ME THE APPROPRIATE ADMINISTRATIVE REQUEST. THIS DISTRICT IS REALLY BACKED UP. HE HASN'T BEEN ABLE TO KEEP UP LATELY...

YOU SHOULD DEFINITELY SEE HIM. HE'LL BE ABLE TO TELL YOU MUCH MORE THAN I CAN. I ONLY KEEP RECORDS RELATING TO MY DISTRICT...

I MUST FIND OUT WHAT HAPPENED. PLEASE TELL ME WHERE I CAN FIND THIS SCULPTRACER.

CERTAINLY... RIGHT NOW HE'S WORKING ON A NEW SCULPTRACE OUTSIDE THE CITY. IT'S LESS THAN THIRTY JUMPS FROM HERE, HEADING TOWARD THE RADAR.

DON'T HESITATE TO COME BACK IF I CAN BE OF FURTHER HELP TO YOU!

IN THE CONTROL ROOM OF THE EJECTOR STATION.

BAD NEWS, SILIS...THE MAN WHO WAS KILLED REALLY WAS AN INSPECTOR. AND THE *SUPER-INSPECTOR* DOESN'T BELIEVE THE DEAD MAN LOST HIS ID RING. THERE'S GOING TO BE AN INVESTIGATION.

OH NO!

HE'S GOING TO SUSPECT ME RIGHT AWAY. I'M RESPONSIBLE FOR SECURITY HERE. HE'S GOING TO SEND THE SYMMETRY KEEPERS AFTER ME...AND THEY ALWAYS MANAGE TO FIND OUT SOMETHING BAD ABOUT YOU!

NO! SILIS, LISTEN TO ME.

WE'LL DEFEND YOU. AFTER ALL, THOSE DEVICES ARE AUTOMATIC.

YOU'RE NOT RESPONSIBLE IF ONE OF THEM DOESN'T WORK.

THEY'LL ACCUSE ME OF HAVING LEFT A HELICUTTER OPEN AFTER A ROUTINE CHECK...

NO!

THEY'LL HAVE TO PROVE THAT. AND EVEN IF THINGS DON'T GO WELL IN COURT, OUR TESTIMONY WILL SHOW EXTENUATING CIRCUMSTANCES.

OH... I KNOW THEY'LL ALL TURN AGAINST ME... I'M IN DEEP TROUBLE!

DON'T WORRY, WE WON'T LET YOU DOWN!

THE SCULPTRACER
IS DOWN THERE.

NO! *HIGHER!*

HIGHER STILL!

EXCUSE ME, I'D LIKE TO... TALK TO YOU FOR A MOMENT.

NO! NOW IT'S TOO MUCH!

I'M A FRIEND OF OLIVE'S AND I'D LIKE...

CAN'T YOU SEE I'M BUSY? YOU CAN TALK TO ME THIS EVENING AT MY STUDIO IN DRAMARD, DISTRICT 44.

I'LL BE THERE.

IT'S STILL TOO MUCH! PAY ATTENTION TO WHAT I'M SAYING!

WHAT COULD HAVE MADE OLIVE FALL FOR SUCH A *BRUTE?*

I HOPE YOU'RE NOT BRINGING ME MORE WORK. JUST LOOK AT THIS! MY ASSISTANT'S BEEN SICK FOR MANY CYCLES AND I CAN'T FIND ANYONE TO REPLACE HIM.

I'D LIKE SOME INFORMATION. I JUST FOUND OUT ABOUT THE DEATH OF A FRIEND. SHE LIVED IN THE 44TH DISTRICT. I'D LIKE TO KNOW WHY SHE KILLED HERSELF.

DON'T EVEN THINK OF ASKING! WE'RE SWORN TO SECRECY.

WE REALIZE THAT WE MUST REMAIN SILENT... AND WHAT'S MORE, I HAVE NO TIME TO WASTE WITH YOU.

I BEG YOU! IT'S VERY IMPORTANT TO ME.

IMPORTANT, IMPORTANT... WELL, HURRY, JUST TELL ME HER NAME. YOU NEVER KNOW...

HER NAME WAS OLIVE. SHE LIVED WITH NATAN, THE SCULPTRACER OF THIS DISTRICT.

I'LL GO LOOK, BUT I REALLY SHOULDN'T. AH, WOMEN! THEY'LL BE MY DOWNFALL.

OLIVE....OLIVE... YOU MEAN OLIVILO?

OLIVILO. I'VE GOT HER SCROLL RIGHT HERE.

SHE HAD A PASSIONATE AFFAIR WITH NATAN...

OLIVE AND NATAN... I CAN'T BELIEVE IT!

BUT THE AFFAIR DIDN'T LAST VERY LONG. THEY WORKED TOGETHER ON CREATING SOME SCULPTRACES AND SOON THEIR RELATIONSHIP SOURED... HE BEGAN TO TREAT HER VERY BADLY... HE HIT HER... SHE DESTROYED HIS SCULPTRACES... HE GOT ANGRY... SHE LEFT HIM... CAME BACK... THEIR FIGHTING INTENSIFIED... NO, NO...I CAN'T TELL YOU ANYTHING MORE. IT'S TOO PERSONAL.

WHAT A HORRIBLE STORY. THAT ANIMAL DESTROYED HER!

WHAT HAPPENED WAS PERFECTLY UNDERSTANDABLE. WHAT WE HAVE HERE IS A SIMPLE MEDIUM AXYSM...IN THE 37TH CYCLE, 23RD PERIOD.

A MEDIUM AXYSM... WHAT'S THAT?

A TEMPORARY AXIS OF SYMMETRY THAT IS ESTABLISHED RIGHT IN THE MIDDLE OF A STORY OR RELATIONSHIP, BETWEEN THE RISE TOWARD LOVE AND THE DESCENT TOWARD HATRED. THE SECOND PART REFERS TO THE INVERSE OF THE FIRST. THE ETERNAL EBB AND FLOW OF TIME... HOW IS IT THAT YOU DON'T ALREADY KNOW THIS?

I'M NOT FROM HERE. I COME FROM ANOTHER PLANET.

ANOTHER PLANET? OH MY! COME UPSTAIRS AND TELL ME ALL ABOUT IT.

SHOW ME YOUR ID RING.

BUT THIS IS AN INSPECTOR'S RING! THAT'S HIGHLY UNUSUAL! WHERE DID YOU FIND IT?

I... I GOT IT FROM A FRIEND...

OH BOY, OH BOY, THAT'S ABSOLUTELY FORBIDDEN! I SHOULD NEVER HAVE SHOWN YOU ALL I HAVE... I'M GOING TO GET INTO A LOT OF *TROUBLE* BECAUSE OF YOU... AH, WOMEN... WOMEN!

I'M SORRY... I DIDN'T KNOW.

YOU MUST SET YOUR RECORD STRAIGHT AS SOON AS POSSIBLE. YOU MUST GET A TOURIST ID RING AND SIGN UP AT A SCROLL COLLECTOR'S OFFICE, AND SO ON... NOW PLEASE GO! HURRY!

OK, OK!

IT MUST BE HERE.

WELL, HERE YOU ARE AGAIN. SO, YOU WERE A FRIEND OF OLIVILO'S?

THEN YOU MUST BE FEEL PASSIONATELY ABOUT SCULPTRACES...

NO. I COULDN'T CARE LESS ABOUT THEM!

THE HOUSES ARE PERFECTLY ADAPTED
TO THE STRANGE PHYSICAL CHARACTERISTICS
OF THIS PLANET. THEY'RE CAREFULLY JOINED
SO AS TO REACT TO THE SMALLEST
FLUCTUATION OF THE THIN PLANETARY CRUST
ON WHICH THEY STAND. IT'S A STRANGE
SENSATION TO FEEL A HOUSE CONTRACT
AND EXPAND AS IF IT WERE BREATHING.

FINALLY!

LUCKY FOR ME, HE LEFT THE AIR VENT OPEN.

I WON'T LEAVE EMPTY-HANDED.

I MUST FINISH WHAT I STARTED. HE WON'T HAVE ANYTHING OF HERS LEFT ONCE I'M THROUGH!

YOU AGAIN!!

WAIT A MINUTE! IF YOU'RE INTERESTED IN FINDING OTHER THINGS, GO TO THE MARKET OF THE DEAD, DISTRICT 1771. EVERYTHING IS THERE!

I'M NOT GOING TO THANK YOU FOR THIS...

WAIT. THAT LOOKS LIKE...

OOOH!

OLIVE'S DIARY, HER SHIRT... THAT MUST BE HER ID RING... I MUST HAVE IT ALL, NO MATTER WHAT THE PRICE!

I WOULD LIKE TO BUY LOT 2332.

ONE MOMENT, PLEASE.

2332, PERSONAL BELONGINGS OF OLIVILO, DECEASED. IS THAT IT?

I'M SORRY. NATAN, THE SCULPTRACER, PURCHASED THAT LOT.

THAT BASTARD! HE TRICKED ME!

WHAT DO YOU WANT FOR ALL OF OLIVE'S BELONGINGS?

THEY'RE *NOT* FOR SALE.

I WANT THEM! THEY'RE VERY IMPORTANT TO ME.

WELL...MAYBE THERE'S A SOLUTION TO THIS...BUT...

BUT WHAT?

YOU COULD WORK FOR ME. YOU COULD CREATE NEW SCULPTRACES TO REPLACE WHAT YOU'VE JUST DESTROYED... BUT IT WON'T BE EASY...

IF OLIVE COULD DO IT, SO CAN I...

COME TO THINK OF IT, I DON'T EVEN KNOW YOUR NAME.

IT'S NELLE.

THAT'S THE NAME OF A REJECT. HERE YOU'LL CALL YOURSELF NELLEN...

WE'LL BEGIN WITH A TORSO. THAT'S THE EASIEST THING TO DO. YOU CAN TAKE OFF YOUR SHIRT.

ALL RIGHT.

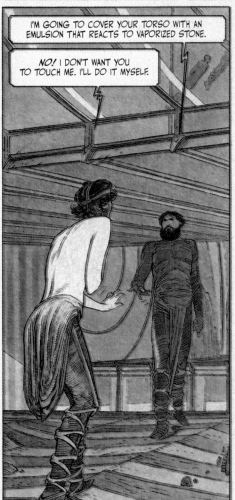

I'M GOING TO COVER YOUR TORSO WITH AN EMULSION THAT REACTS TO VAPORIZED STONE.

NO! I DON'T WANT YOU TO TOUCH ME. I'LL DO IT MYSELF.

AS YOU PLEASE.

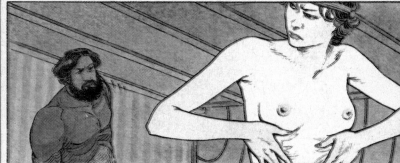

YOU'LL SLOWLY PASS THROUGH A CLOUD OF VAPORIZED STONE. AS YOU MOVE, I'LL DISPATCH A SERIES OF ELECTRIC CHARGES TO SOLIDIFY THE VAPORS.

GO AHEAD.

TSSSS...

JUST LOOK AT THAT! THE GESTURE IS TENSE AND RESTRAINED! YOU'RE HOLDING BACK, AND YOU DIDN'T SPREAD THE EMULSION PROPERLY...

WE'RE GOING TO TRY AGAIN. BUT THIS TIME WITH THE WHOLE BODY!

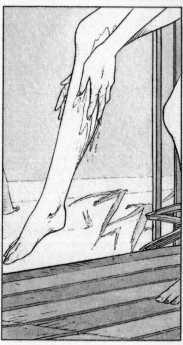

155

YOU CAN GO AHEAD.

NO! YOU'RE AS STIFF AS A RAMROD.

THAT WAS JUST AS BAD. IT'S HOPELESS... OH, YOU SHOUL HAVE SEEN YOUR FRIEND OLIVILO. SHE WAS SPECTACULAR...

SURE. AND IF YOU HADN'T PUSHED HER TO HER DEATH, YOU COULD STILL BE EXPLOITING HER!

OUT! I'VE HAD ENOUGH OF YOU !

BASTARD! BASTARD! BASTARD!

AHHH!

CALM DOWN, NELLEN... CALM DOWN...

THERE...THAT'S BETTER... YOU'RE EXHAUSTED... HOW LONG HAS IT BEEN SINCE YOU LAST SLEPT?

VERY WELL! YOU'LL START BY TAKING A REST. EVERYTHING THAT YOU NEED IS HERE.

NO, I WANT TO GO ON RIGHT NOW. I WANT TO DO IT!

BEGINNINGS ARE ALWAYS DIFFICULT. HAVE CONFIDENCE IN YOURSELF AND EVERYTHING WILL WORK OUT...

YES! YES! GO ON! THAT'S MUCH BETTER, NELLEN!

YOU SEE, THE SCULPTRACE IS MUCH MORE DEFINED.

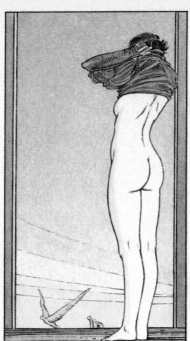

158

THAT MASSAGE WAS GREAT...
YOUR HANDS ARE SO LARGE...
I WOULD NEVER HAVE THOUGHT....

RELAX!

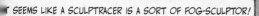
IT SEEMS LIKE A SCULPTRACER IS A SORT OF FOG-SCULPTOR!

NO, IT'S COMPLETELY DIFFERENT. SCULPTRACING IS THE DECOMPOSITION OF A MOVEMENT ACCORDING TO THE RHYTHM OF THE HEARTBEAT.

IT'S MOVEMENT FIXED FOREVER IN STONE...

A FOG SCULPTURE IS JUST A COPY OF A BODY WITHOUT MOVEMENT... THERE'S NO SIMILARITY BETWEEN THE TWO.

GOOD. WE'LL CONTINUE TOMORROW. YOU'RE EXHAUSTED.

NELLEN, IF YOU REALLY WANT TO PICK UP OLIVILO'S THINGS, HERE'S THE TITLE DEED.

BUT...I'VE ONLY JUST STARTED WORKING FOR YOU.

THE SOONER YOU GET OLIVILO'S ID RING, THE BETTER. YOU'RE IN GREAT DANGER NOW.

OH, SO YOU KNOW ABOUT THAT, TOO!

THERE'S SOMETHING I MUST KNOW... WHAT REALLY HAPPENED BETWEEN YOU AND OLIVE?

NATAN! I HAVE TO KNOW!

PLEASE ANSWER ME!

HERE IT IS.

2332... IT'S THE LOT OF NATAN, THE SCULPTRACER.

THERE. IT'S OPEN.

I'LL HAVE TROUBLE RESISTING HIS CHARM... IT'LL BE DIFFICULT NOT TO TRUST HIM...

AT LAST!!

NATAN ISN'T THE KIND OF MAN I IMAGINED. I WAS WRONG ABOUT HIM...

WOW!

SHE WROTE DOWN EVERYTHING SINCE SHE ARRIVED ON ZARA.

HUNDREDS OF PAGES. IT'LL TAKE ME A WHILE TO READ ALL THIS.

THE NEXT DAY.

THIS IS THE FIRST FULL NIGHT'S SLEEP I'VE HAD SINCE I ARRIVED.

I COULD START POLISHING THAT IF YOU WANT.

BE CAREFUL. SOME PARTS ARE STILL VERY FRAGILE.

CRRRR2!

OH, I'M SORRY!

I'D LIKE TO ASK YOU SOMETHING ABOUT OLIVE.

LATER, NELLEN, LATER...

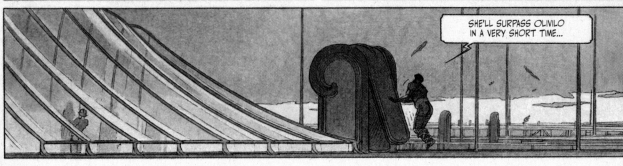

164

I CAN'T STAND THESE SCULPTRACES ANYMORE...THEY'RE THE ONLY THINGS THAT EXIST FOR HIM... HE LOOKS AT ME AS IF I WERE MADE OF VAPORIZED STONE... I MUST DO SOMETHING.

CHAPTER II'

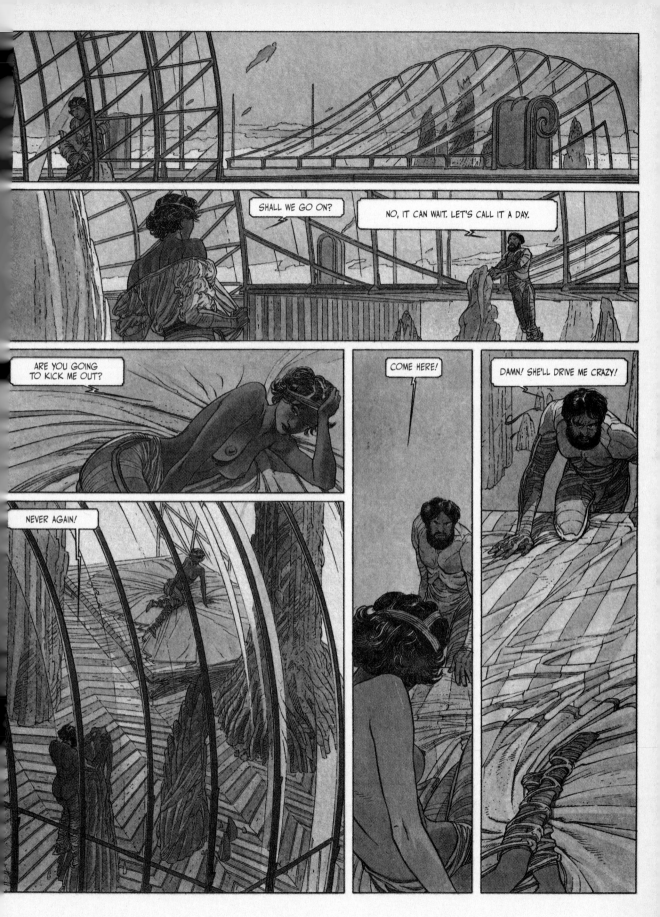

YES! CONTINUE!

A PART OF OLIVE IS ALIVE AGAIN...

NOW, EVERYTHING IS BACK TO NORMAL...

LITTLE BY LITTLE, I'M DISCOVERING ALL THAT WENT ON BETWEEN YOU AND OLIVE.

THE IDEA THAT I'M GOING TO RELIVE WHAT SHE WENT THROUGH WITH YOU MAKES ME UNEASY.

YES, IT'S A CLASSIC AXYSM.

SO I'LL REALLY BE RELIVING EXACTLY THE SAME THINGS?

NO... IT'S NEVER EXACTLY THE SAME. IT'S MORE LIKE A NATURAL MIRROR, LIKE THE LANDSCAPE REFLECTED ON THE SURFACE OF A LAKE.

THE WATER IS NEVER PERFECTLY STILL. THE SLIGHTEST BREEZE CHANGES THE REFLECTION. IT CAN SOMETIMES ALTER IT SO MUCH THAT IT'S UNRECOGNIZABLE...

HOWEVER, EVEN THE SMALLEST PARTICLES OF THE LANDSCAPE ARE REFLECTED ON THAT SURFACE.

THEN I HOPE MY REFLECTION WILL BE VERY ALTERED.

I'M LIVING IN YOUR DISTRICT NOW, SO I'VE COME TO REGISTER MYSELF ON YOUR LISTS. I'D LIKE MY PAPERS TO BE IN ORDER AS SOON AS POSSIBLE.

WE'LL SEE ABOUT THAT. FIRST OF ALL, I HAVE TO CHECK YOUR ID RING. I DON'T WANT ANY TROUBLE.

PERFECT. IT'S A NORMAL TOURIST ID. HOW DID YOU GET IT?

FROM A FRIEND WHO...

IT'S NOT IMPORTANT...LET'S GO DOWNSTAIRS. WE'LL REGISTER YOU.

WE'LL SET UP A SCROLL FOR YOU. IT MUST BE UPDATED EVERY TIME PERIOD... YOU CAN ASK SOMEONE TO HELP YOU IN THE BEGINNING IF YOU NEED TO.

GOOD...

BZZZT, BZZZT.

JUST A MOMENT, PLEASE.

THIS IS THE SUPER-INTENDENT IN CHARGE OF THE INVESTIGATION OF THE DEATH OF INSPECTOR "S."

SOMEONE TOLD ME YOU WERE GOING TO CALL. I CAREFULLY EXAMINED THE AXYSM OF THE ENTIRE LIFE OF "S." THERE'S NOTHING THAT CAN BE CONSIDERED SYMMETRICAL TO HIS DEATH.

IT'S ALL THE SAME AS FAR AS I CAN SEE. NOW YOU MUST FIND OUT WHO'S RESPONSIBLE TO RE-ESTABLISH THE SYMMETRY.

I THOUGHT SO. IT'S A "BROKEN MIRROR." WHETHER ACCIDENTAL OR NOT STILL REMAINS TO BE SEEN.

OH MY!

I'D BE GLAD TO SEND THE CULPRIT THROUGH THE HELICUTTER MYSELF!

HA, HA... I'M NOT SURPRISED SUPERINTENDENT... GOOD-BYE.

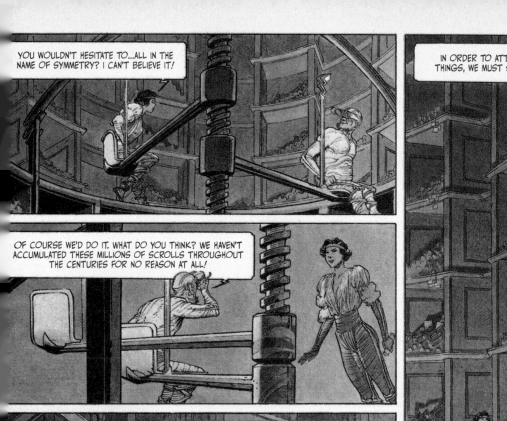

YOU WOULDN'T HESITATE TO...ALL IN THE NAME OF SYMMETRY? I CAN'T BELIEVE IT!

IN ORDER TO ATTAIN A HIGHER ORDER OF THINGS, WE MUST SET EXTREME STANDARDS.

OF COURSE WE'D DO IT. WHAT DO YOU THINK? WE HAVEN'T ACCUMULATED THESE MILLIONS OF SCROLLS THROUGHOUT THE CENTURIES FOR NO REASON AT ALL!

YOU STILL HAVE A LOT TO LEARN, MY DEAR GAMMA. JUST REMEMBER THAT SYMMETRY IS HIGHLY VALUED HERE... AT ANY COST...

THAT'S THE PRICE WE HAVE TO PAY FOR RAISING OUR LEVEL OF EXISTENCE TO THE POINT WHERE ALL THINGS BECOME TRANSPARENT...

THAT'S IT...I'M NOW IN THE RECORDS. YOU COULD HELP ME FILL OUT MY SCROLL. I DON'T REALLY KNOW WHAT TO PUT IN IT.

IT'S EASY...

YOU'LL SAY THAT YOU LIVED THROUGH A PERIOD OF HATE AND DESTRUCTION, THEN THROUGH A PERIOD OF LOVE AND CREATIVITY. IT'LL ALL BE IN PERFECT SYMMETRY WITH WHAT I EXPERIENCED WITH OLIVILO.

BUT THEN OUR RELATIONSHIP WILL END SOON...

YES, OF COURSE.

PERHAPS YOU'RE GOING TO REJECT ME THE WAY YOU DID OLIVE...

NO, I'M SURE YOU'LL LEAVE JUST AS YOU ARRIVED... WHENEVER YOU WISH...

NEVER! HOW CAN YOU BE SO *CERTAIN?*

IT'S INEVITABLE!

AND YOU'RE GOING TO ACCEPT THAT WITHOUT A FIGHT?

OF COURSE. THE WAY I ACCEPT THE SUNSET AND THE DAWN...

DISCUSSING THIS TOPIC IS HOPELESS... I'M GOING TO PROVE TO HIM THAT ALL THESE RULES BASED ON SYMMETRY HAVE NOTHING TO DO WITH ME!

AS TIME GOES BY, HE'LL HAVE TO FACE THE EVIDENCE.

BUT STILL, HOW CAN HE ACCEPT THIS SO READILY AFTER ALL THAT HAS HAPPENED BETWEEN US?

YOU'RE IN A BAD SPOT, SILIS... ALL THE EVIDENCE IS AGAINST YOU.

BUT, I SWEAR I WON'T LET THEM WALK ALL OVER ME!

WE'LL SUCCEED IN PROVING YOUR GUILT. AND SINCE YOU'RE DENYING EVERYTHING, THE COURT WON'T CONSIDER EXTENUATING CIRCUMSTANCES IN YOUR DEFENSE.

THEY'RE ACCUSING YOU OF HAVING LEFT THE HELICUTTER OPEN AFTER A ROUTINE MAINTENANCE CHECK.

NO!

THE DAY THE INSPECTOR WAS KILLED, YOU DIDN'T ACTIVATE THE SECURITY MECHANISM.

YOU MUST HAVE PUSHED THIS LEVER, THUS TURNING ON THE HELICUTTER.

NO, NO! LISTEN TO ME!

SHUT UP! WE'RE GOING TO CHECK EVERY ASPECT OF YOUR LIFE. WE'RE GOING TO TURN YOU OVER TO THE SYMMETRY KEEPERS... THEY ALWAYS FIND SOMETHING WE CAN USE!

FOR HEAVEN'S SAKE, LISTEN TO ME!

YOU'RE MAKING A BIG *MISTAKE!* YOU PULL THE LEVER TOWARD YOU IF YOU WANT TO TURN OFF THE HELICUTTER,

OH NO!

YES, I RECOGNIZE YOU. CAN I BE OF FURTHER HELP?

SINCE YOU'VE TOLD ME ABOUT THE DEATH OF MY FRIEND, OLIVE, I HAVEN'T STOPPED THINKING ABOUT IT. I'M TRYING TO UNDERSTAND HER REASONS FOR COMMITTING SUICIDE... IT'S STILL NOT CLEAR TO ME...

I FOUND HER DIARY. THERE ARE NO ENTRIES AROUND THE 14TH PERIOD BEFORE HER DEATH, WHICH IS WHEN SHE LEFT NATAN, THE SCULPTRACER...

DURING THAT TIME SHE MUST HAVE LIVED SOMEWHERE, AND SIGNED UP WITH ANOTHER KEEPER. COULD YOU HELP ME FIND HIM?

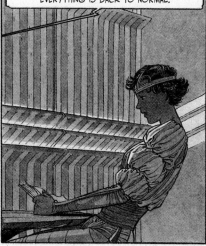

YOU'RE OUT OF LUCK! I RECEIVED A FORMAL REQUEST FOR INFORMATION ABOUT HER... THIS DISTRICT HAS BEEN A LITTLE BEHIND SCHEDULE, BUT NOW EVERYTHING IS BACK TO NORMAL.

I'VE JUST SENT ALL HER RECORDS TO THE CHIEF SYMMETRY KEEPER, SO THAT HE CAN PROCEED WITH A FULL VERIFICATION OF HER STATUS. I'M SORRY.

I'VE GOT TO FIND OUT ALL THAT HAPPENED DURING THE LAST DAYS OF HER LIFE, AND WHY SHE DECIDED TO KILL HERSELF...

I MUST FIND OUT THE TRUTH!

NO!

NO, NEVER HEARD OF HER.

SHE CAME HERE SOME TIME AGO. SINCE IT'S A MATTER OF PUBLIC RECORD, I'M FREE TO TELL YOU ALL I KNOW. SHE WAS GOING TO MEET SOME FLITTERS OUTSIDE THE PLANET'S SURFACE.

THEN SHE'S STILL ALIVE! THAT'S WONDERFUL NEWS!!

YES... I THINK I REMEMBER SOMETHING ABOUT HER. WAIT A MOMENT, PLEASE...

I UNDERSTAND EVERYTHING NOW... THE FLITTERS COULDN'T LAND ON DRAMARD...THEY'RE REJECTS. WHEN OLIVE JUMPED OFF THE PLANET TO JOIN THEM, EVERYBODY BELIEVED SHE'D COMMITTED SUICIDE.

...I'LL NEVER GET USED TO THIS UPSIDE-DOWN WORLD. TOO BAD NELLE DIDN'T WANT TO COME WITH ME ON THIS TRIP. WE'RE SO STRONG WHEN WE'RE TOGETHER. NOW IT'S TOO LATE - THERE'S ONLY ONE WAY TO ESCAPE THIS MIRROR-IMAGE DESTINY. THE GREAT LEAP.

CHAPTER 1'

YES, SUPER-INSPECTOR, ALL THIS EVIDENCE SHOWS THAT THESE POOR PEOPLE WERE THE VICTIMS OF A TECHNICAL FAILURE...IN SYMMETRY WITH THE DEATH OF INSPECTOR "S."

HMM...ARE YOU SURE? AND WHAT DO YOU THINK, SILIS?

A TECH - TECHNICAL FAILURE. NO DOUBT ABOUT IT!

ANOTHER CHECKPOINT. IT'S GETTING ANNOYING!

OLIVILO, TOURIST: ALL IS IN ORDER!

I MUST FIND THE PEOPLE WHO HELPED OLIVE ESCAPE. SOME OF THEM MUST LIVE NEAR THE REJECT VILLAGE. I'M SURE THEY'LL HELP ME.

NATAN WAS RIGHT. IT'S INCREDIBLE, BUT MY EXPERIENCE WILL BE SYMMETRICAL, AFTER ALL. I DON'T REALLY HAVE THE HEART TO SAY GOOD-BYE. HE'LL UNDERSTAND...

I'VE COME TO NOTIFY YOU THAT I'LL BE LEAVING DRAMARD FOR ANOTHER HOLLOW PLANET.

WHICH DISTRICT DO YOU BELONG TO?

NUMBER 1221. I'D LIKE TO THANK ALL THE COLLECTORS WHO'VE HELPED ME FIND OUT WHAT HAPPENED TO MY FRIEND.

MUCH OBLIGED!

VLAM

EXCUSE ME, WHERE'S THE EJECTOR FOR THE REJECT VILLAGE?

IT'S ON THE OTHER SIDE, BETWEEN DISTRICT 3773 AND 858.

I'M GOING TO SEE OLIVE AGAIN!!

CONTINUING THE INVESTIGATION AMONG THE REJECTS STARTED BY INSPECTOR "S" WON'T BE EASY...

THE HYPERINSPECTOR IS WATCHING ME CLOSELY... THERE'D BETTER NOT BE ANOTHER BLUNDER.

HEY, WATCH WHERE YOU'RE GOING!!

OH, I'M SORRY.

EXCUSE ME, BUT I DIDN'T SEE YOU COMING... YOU'RE PROBABLY GOING TO THE REJECT VILLAGE TO INVESTIGATE THE DISAPPEARANCE OF CERTAIN SHIPMENTS...

WHAT THE....! HOW DID YOU KNOW THAT! MY MISSION IS TOP SECRET.

I SEE ONLY ONE POSSIBLE EXPLANATION: YOU MUST HAVE TRAVELED SOME TIME AGO WITH MY PREDECESSOR AND YOU MUST HAVE STOLEN HIS ID RING. SHOW ME YOUR RING!

IT'S A REGULAR TOURIST ID. I DON'T SEE ANYTHING WRONG WITH IT... YOU MUST HAVE WORKED THIS OUT PRETTY WELL...

ANYWAY, THE CASE IS ALREADY CLOSED. THE DEATH OF INSPECTOR "S" HAS BEEN CLASSIFIED AS TECHNICAL FAILURE. BUT I KNOW BETTER, I'M NO IDIOT!

HE'S GIVING ME WARNING...

WE'RE ALMOST THERE...

I WANT YOU TO COME WITH ME SO I CAN QUESTION YOU TOGETHER WITH THE REJECTS. BUT BEFORE THAT, I MUST TAKE CARE OF SOMETHING HERE...

I HAVE NOTHING TO FEAR FROM A CONFRONTATION. THE WHOLE THING SHOULD HAPPEN THE SAME WAY AS WHEN I LEFT...

THAT'S...IT...THEY...ARE...BACK...SAID...THEY...WOULD...BE...

SAVED...AT...LAST...

COME...WITH...ME...NOW...THEY...WILL...TAKE...CARE...
OF...YOU... YOU'LL...SEE...

THANK...YOU...YOU...ARE...
SAVING...MY...LIFE...

I DON'T UNDERSTAND.
I CAN ACCEPT THAT ALL
THESE PEOPLE LIVE SYMMETRICAL
EXPERIENCES...BUT HOW DID I BECOME
SUBJECT TO THE SAME LAWS?

THERE ARE TWO POSSIBLE EXPLANATIONS:
EITHER SYMMETRY IS A FUNDAMENTAL LAW OF
NATURE...BUT IN THAT CASE, WHY WOULD
SYMMETRY KEEPERS NEED TO EXIST?

OR IT'S A HUMAN CONVENTION CREATED BY A DEVIOUS MIND...
BUT HOW COULD IT EXERCISE COMPLETE CONTROL OVER
THE MAJORITY OF THE INHABITANTS OF THIS PLANET?

NO, I DON'T LIKE EITHER OF THOSE EXPLANATIONS...
EVEN I, WHO DON'T WANT TO, FIND MYSELF
OBEYING THE LAWS OF SYMMETRY...

WHAT IF IT ALL WAS JUST AN ILLUSION, A SLIGHT DISTORTION OF MEMORY...WHICH WOULD MAKE THINGS APPEAR THE OPPOSITE OF WHAT ONE IS EXPERIENCING...

OR BETTER STILL, SINCE ALL THE NAMES, NUMBERS, MEASURES, AND ALL THEIR SCIENTIFIC PRINCIPLES ARE BASED ON SYMMETRY, THIS COULD HAVE SLOWLY INFLUENCED EVEN THE LEAST IMPORTANT OF THEIR ACTIONS...

WELL, I'VE COME UP WITH FOUR DIFFERENT EXPLANATIONS, TWO OF WHICH ARE THE OPPOSITE OF THE OTHER TWO. YET ANOTHER INSTANCE OF THEIR DAMN SYMMETRY! MY THOUGHT PATTERNS HAVE BECOME SYMMETRICAL... THIS STRANGE WORLD HAS CONFUSED ME COMPLETELY. IT'S HIGH TIME THAT I LEFT.

IS...THERE... ANY...

PIECE... MISSING...?

NO... MY...LORD...

EVERY...THING... IS...HERE...

WERE...YOU...IN...THAT...POSITION...LAST...TIME...

YES...YES...

IT'S STILL FROZEN!

ON ZARA, MY PLANET, WE AREN'T CONSTRAINED BY RULES OF SYMMETRY. YOU PROBABLY CAN'T IMAGINE HOW MUCH FREEDOM WE HAVE.

I KNOW. THAT'S WHAT THE REJECTS SAY.

WHY HAVEN'T YOU TRIED TO INTEGRATE THE REJECTS INTO YOUR SOCIETY?

WE DID TRY. MANY GENERATIONS AGO. OUR ANCESTORS NAIVELY BELIEVED THAT THEY COULD RESTORE THE SYMMETRY OF ASYMMETRICAL PHYSIQUES BY CUTTING OFF THE IRREGULAR PARTS. IT WAS A TERRIBLE FAILURE.

OUR ANCESTORS REALIZED THAT SYMMETRY WAS FIRST AND FOREMOST A SPIRITUAL MATTER, A MENTAL STATE...

THEY DECIDED THAT CHAOS SHOULD BALANCE OUT OUR ORDER... CHAOS AND DISORDER ARE WHAT THE REJECTS ARE ALL ABOUT...

THE REJECTS HAVE GAINED A CERTAIN AMOUNT OF FREEDOM BECAUSE OF THIS...

AND YOU MADE THEM PAY A HIGH PRICE FOR IT.

WATCH OUT, WE'RE GOING TO TRY TO SURPRISE THEM.

NO, DON'T DO THAT!

WELL...
I... NEVER

WHY DID YOU DO THAT?

IT WAS THEM OR ME.
DON'T YOU REALIZE THAT?

LOOK, I WAS RIGHT.
ALL THE STOLEN GOODS
ARE RIGHT HERE.

YOU'RE *CRAZY!*
DON'T COUNT ON
MY HELP ANYMORE...

?

GOOD-BYE,
INSPECTOR.

WHAT...WILL...WE...DO...NOW...
MY...LORD...?

OH...MY...MY...MY...

I'M THE CHIEF SPECTOR - YOU'RE GOING TO HEAR ABOUT ME!

A SPECIAL TASK FORCE WILL BE HERE SOON. I'M GOING BACK TO DRAMARD.

I WAS SURE THIS MISSION WOULD BE SUCCESSFUL. I FAILED TO SUCCEED IN A SIMILAR ONE SOME TIME AGO...

IN A CERTAIN SENSE, THAT YOUNG FOREIGNER AND THE REJECTS ARE BOTH RIGHT, OUR SYMMETRICAL POSTULATES ALMOST ELIMINATE THE ADVENTUROUS ASPECTS OF OUR JOBS.

NOTHING IS MORE BORING THAN KNOWING WHAT'S GOING TO HAPPEN TO YOU...

ACTUALLY, SYMMETRY IS A STUPID PRINCIPLE. IT'S LIKE BEING FORCED TO REPLICATE EVERYTHING IN REVERSE ORDER.

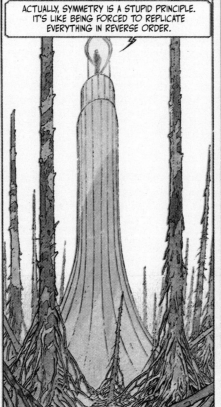

IT'S LIKE CREATING A DOUBLE OF EVERYTHING, THE ORIGINAL AND A PLAGIARIZED COPY...

THOSE PEOPLE ARE INFINITELY FREER THAN WE ARE, DESPITE THEIR SLOWNESS AND INCOMPETENCE...

I'D BENEFIT FROM KNOWING THEM A LITTLE BETTER. I'VE THE FEELING THAT I'LL BE GOING THERE MORE OFTEN...

AS A MATTER OF FACT, I'VE ALWAYS LIKED REJECTS...THEIR CHRONIC ASYMMETRY NEVER CEASES TO FASCINATE ME...

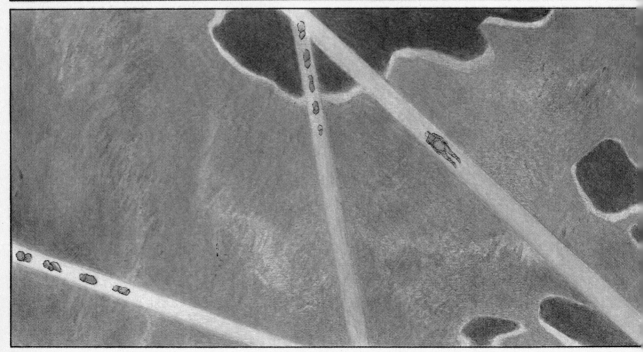

EPOCH 139, 35TH CYCLE, 43RD PERIOD

TODAY I DECIDED TO START A NEW DIARY.
I LEFT THE LAST ONE ON NOGEGON.
I NO LONGER HAVE THE STRENGTH TO
RETURN AND LOOK FOR IT AT NATAN'S -
HE'S CRAZY. I REALLY REGRET HAVING LEFT
SUCH A PERSONAL OBJECT WITH HIM.
AFTER A SHORT TRIP, I ARRIVED ON VEDRA,
THE SIXTH PLANET IN THE HOLLOW
GROUNDS SYSTEM. I'M MOST SURPRISED
BY THE OVERPOWERING GRAVITY -
EVERYTHING IS HEAVY HERE. OLIVILO
IS DEAD, BUT OLIVE IS VERY MUCH ALIVE...

THE END

LOOK FOR THESE BOOKS FROM HUMANOIDS/DC COMICS:

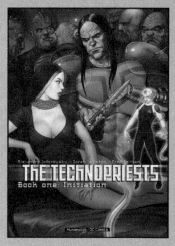

THE TECHNOPRIESTS Vol.1: Initiation
Softcover. 160 pages
Written by Alexandro Jodorowsky with art by
Zoran Janjetov and Fred Beltran

The bastard son of a pirate, the young boy
called Albino has only one goal, to become a
member of the Technoguild and free the
minds of every citizen in the galaxy, or die
trying. And he just might! The path to
become a Technopriest is a difficult one and
Albino must face many trials before he can
fulfill his destiny. INITIATION tells the story of
Albino's first three years of training to
become a member of the powerful
Technoguild.

TOWNSCAPES
Softcover. 176 pages
Written by Pierre Christin and illustrated by
Enki Bilal with colors by Dan Brown

In the TOWNSCAPES collection, Bilal collabo-
rates with writer Pierre Christin to tell three
tales of modern day towns caught up in fantastic circumstances: THE CRUISE OF LOST
SOULS, SHIP OF STONE and THE TOWN
THAT DIDN'T EXIST. Each story presents a
timeless tale set in the trappings of the pres-
ent, with a yearning towards the fables of
yesterday.

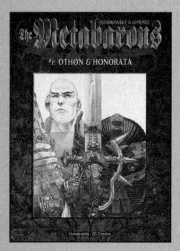

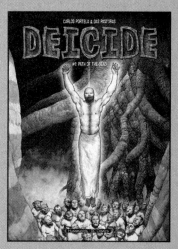

THE METABARONS Vol. 1: Othon & Honorata
Softcover. 136 pages
Written by Alexandro Jodorowsky and illus-
trated by Juan Gimenez

Learn the story of the ultimate bloodline of
warriors as the history of the Metabaron's
clan unfolds. This first collection introduces
the Metabaron's ancestors and reveals their
origins. Find out the source of the family's
vast wealth. Learn why every Metabaron has
cybernetic implants and why the only way to
become the next Metabaron is to defeat your
own father in mortal combat. Gimenez's lav-
ish artwork fills every page with a stunning
combination of action and drama, telling one
of the most unique stories in comics today.

DEICIDE Vol. 1: Path of the Dead
Softcover. 112 pages
Written by Carlos Portela and illustrated by
Das Pastoras

Agon, a great hunter and warrior, lives in a
world where tribal villagers pay bloody sacri-
fices to a seemingly never-ending pantheon
of both good and evil gods. Angered by the
unnecessary sacrifice of his love, Aldara, to
the hideous god Madorak, Agon rejects the
gods and sets out on a journey to reclaim
Aldara's soul. Along the way, Agon is aided
and sometimes hindered by Beluch, a lion-
headed man with problems of his own.

THE HORDE
Softcover. 144 pages
Written and illustrated by Igor Baranko with
colors by Dave Stewart and Charlie Kirchoff

In the year 1206, Genghis Khan and his
Golden Horde dominated an immense terri-
tory from the Pacific Ocean to the Caspian
Sea with only 150,000 men. In the year 2040,
the newest Russian dictator has a unique
vision: to invoke the spirit of Genghis Khan
and his Golden Horde and create a vast
empire reaching from the Pacific Ocean to
the Atlantic. Only the last Chechen, survivor
of a nuclear holocaust and host for Shiva, the
great destroyer, can stand in his way!

Humanoids / DC Comics